A ROBERT STIGWOOD
IN ASSOCIATION WITH
OF
A FILM BY MICHA

PETER FRAM
THE BEE GEES

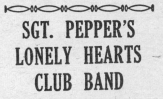

SGT. PEPPER'S LONELY HEARTS CLUB BAND

Starring

FRANKIE HOWERD • PAUL NICHOLAS

DONALD PLEASENCE

introducing
SANDY FARINA as Strawberry Fields • DIANNE STEINBERG as Lucy
and STEVE MARTIN as Dr. Maxwell Edison

Special Guest Stars
AEROSMITH • ALICE COOPER • EARTH, WIND & FIRE • BILLY PRESTON
and GEORGE BURNS as Mr. Kite

Music and Lyrics by JOHN LENNON and PAUL McCARTNEY
"Here Comes The Sun" by GEORGE HARRISON

Director of Photography OWEN ROEMAN ASC • Associate Producer BILL OAKES
Executive in Charge of Production ROGER M. ROTHSTEIN

Choreography by PATRICIA BIRCH
Music Arranged and Directed by GEORGE MARTIN
Written by HENRY EDWARDS
Story by HENRY EDWARDS and ROBERT STIGWOOD
Executive Producer DEE ANTHONY
Produced by ROBERT STIGWOOD • Directed by MICHAEL SCHULTZ

SGT. PEPPER'S LONELY HEARTS CLUB BAND

a novel by

HENRY EDWARDS

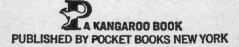
A KANGAROO BOOK
PUBLISHED BY POCKET BOOKS NEW YORK

Distributed in Canada by PaperJacks Ltd., a Licensee
of the trademarks of Simon & Schuster, a division of
Gulf+Western Corporation.

Another *Original* publication of POCKET BOOKS

POCKET BOOKS, a Simon & Schuster division of
GULF & WESTERN CORPORATION
1230 Avenue of the Americas, New York, N.Y. 10020

In Canada distributed by PaperJacks Ltd.,
330 Steelcase Road, Markham, Ontario.

ISBN: 0-671-82211-X

First Pocket Books printing July, 1978

Trademarks registered in the United States and other countries.

Interior design by Sofia Grunfeld

Printed in Canada

SGT. PEPPER'S
LONELY HEARTS
CLUB BAND

ONE

*The small provincial town of Pomme de la
Pomme—the south of France—Winter, 1915*

Bombs! Death! Destruction! Has there ever been
a war as fierce as World War I? Has there ever
been a battle as severe as the Battle of Pomme
de la Pomme? This battle was as fierce as the
Battle of Verdun, as destructive as the Battle of
Lenberg, as dangerous as the Battle of the Marne,
as exhausting as the Battle of the Somme, as grue-
some as the Battle of Gallipoli. It was the most
severe battle of all!

The eyes and ears of the world are focused on
this ravaged French village of Pomme de la
Pomme, whose houses and barns have toppled to
the ground and whose once lush fields have now
turned to mud.

Determined to fight to the death to gain control of Pomme de la Pomme, the Allies and the

Axis have relentlessly used guns, tanks, grenades, as well as all the other horrors of modern warfare, to annihilate the other side.

Each day at the crack of dawn, they would stealthily crawl toward each other. Their teeth clenched, their eyes narrowed to tiny slits, they would get so close they could smell each other's sweat. Too close! They would retreat back until they were far enough away to begin again. Gain an inch! Lose an inch! No wonder the fighting had raged on for twenty-one long days and twenty-one even longer nights.

The Red Cross, the Big Sisters, even a handful of Brownies on an educational exchange program, had braved the dangers of the front line to do what they could for the war-torn soldiers of the Battle of Pomme de la Pomme. Still, the supplies had to run out—they did! The food had to run out—it did! The water had to run out—it did! The fuel had to run out—it did! The ammunition had to run out—it did!

What could the soldiers do? They wearily climbed from the filthy, cold trenches to engage each other in man-to-man combat. They fought, bit, and wrestled each other to the ground.

When would it all end?

On the twenty-second day, at exactly ten past noon, off in the distance, there was the faint tinkling sound of a marching band. The sound immediately riveted the ear. One by one, the weary soldiers lifted their bedraggled heads. The lively music made them smile; they began to tap their toes in time to the infectious rhythm. Suddenly, all they wanted to do was turn somersaults and laugh.

Their heads turned in the direction of the

music. And what did they see? *Sgt. Pepper's Lonely Hearts Club Band!*

Hundreds upon hundreds of happy, singing, dancing soldiers marched behind the band—men from all countries, walks of life, religions and races marching side by side in complete and perfect joy.

"I am so-o very happy!" announced a Frenchman. "This is even better than April in Paris!"

"It is good, this music," observed a German. "It is better than Munich during the Oktoberfest."

"Ha! Ha! I love to laugh. It has been a very long time!" trilled an Italian. "This beats driving a Maserati through all the traffic lights in Rome!"

"This is most wonderful!" stated an Englishman. "It's more jolly than Hyde Park on a sunny Sunday afternoon."

For the first time in nearly a month, the soldiers could see a sky of blue.

Sgt. Pepper's Lonely Hearts Club Band had done it again. Who were these musicians who could make peace out of war? They were good American boys—each and every one.

The leader of the band, Sgt. Phineas Patrick Paul Pepper, was a young farming lad from the small town of Heartland, U.S.A. He had always been a happy boy with a smile like sunshine and a heart as big as the universe. The only son of Harry and Elinor Pepper, two humble farmers, he had been taught from earliest childhood the Heartland way: "Kindness above all else!"

Bass drummer Manfred Small, cornetist Jack Porter, and saxophonist Eddie Carter were just as kind, generous, and decent.

Sgt. Pepper's Lonely Hearts Club Band played

in trenches and on top of tanks; they played for
the wounded and the homesick. Everywhere they
played, peace and friendship reigned supreme.

One brisk fall morning, a parade was held for
them on the fabled French boulevard, the Champs
Elysées. At the end of it stood the Joint Chiefs of
Staff, ready to award Pepper the highest honor
the United States Army had to give: the Purple
Staff for Distinguished Music-Making in the Line
of Duty.

The gleaming medal was hung around Phineas'
neck.

No Heartland boy had ever been awarded such
an honor before.

Phineas blushed scarlet-red as he received a
twenty-one-gun salute.

"Vive le Pepper!" cheered the thousands of
merry French people lining the grand boulevard.

Sgt. Pepper's blush grew even deeper. The only
way he could repay these good people was to make
them feel as wonderful as he could. The only way
to make them feel that wonderful was to lift his
baton.

"Oooh, la, la!" screamed the crowd. And suddenly there was dancing in the streets! Total
strangers embraced each other. They waltzed; they
polkaed; they jumped up and down. It was an
amazing sight.

The day of Sgt. Pepper's return from the Great
War had been declared a town holiday by Mr.
Kite, the newly elected Mayor of Heartland.

That morning, all of Heartland waited anxiously
on the porches of their frame houses—carefully
painted in pastel greens, pinks, and blues—with
white picket fences and swings on the front

porches. In each Heartland yard there was one large tree with a tree house on top of it built by a Heartland dad. And in each basement was stored an ice-cream freezer packed full with homemade peppermint ice-cream, Heartland's favorite summertime treat.

Heartlanders took Sgt. Pepper's return as a time to review their blessings—and of blessings they had many. They were all glad to be Heartlanders. At the moment of birth, each had been kissed instead of slapped, and each had grown up to be there before a neighbor need even ask for help.

The heart of Heartland was a rectangular town square. On the south side of it, side by side were the Heartland Confectionery Bakery, the First National Bank of Heartland, the Learning-Is-Happiness Bookshop, the Heartland Post Office and the Heartland General Store.

The entire north side was taken up by Heartland City Hall, where Mr. Kite made his offices.

He had been elected on the Progressive ticket and had run on a platform of more sunshine, love and kindness. The Heartlanders loved this sprightly little man. They were proud that such a loving man had been elected Mayor.

The east side of Heartland's town square was occupied by the Lovely Hair Salon, the Heartland Home for Our Beloved Aged, run by Mr. and Mrs. Stuart Fields, the Heartland Café and the Heartland Sweet Shoppe.

The Heartland combination Elementary and High School and Heartland Playground occupied all of the west side.

Directly in the center of Heartland town square stood the Heartland bandstand. This is where Sgt.

Pepper's Lonely Hearts Club Band played before they had ever been called to war!

But now the war was over. All of Heartland eagerly awaited Phineas' return.

It is precisely 12:02 in the afternoon. The main city train chugs into Heartland Depot and the beloved Sergeant steps off it. The crowd goes wild. Pepper is hoisted onto the shoulders of his friends and neighbors and carried into town—a conquering hero come home to roost.

On the bandstand, Phineas signs autographs and poses for pictures for the *Heartland Gazette* with his wife, Abigail, and their baby daughter, Saralinda. Phineas and Abigail had fallen in love at a high school dance where Phineas was leading the school band. All the girls loved Phineas and his music, but Phineas saw in Abigail a special quality the other girls lacked. She was quiet and soft-spoken and not taken to giggling. Phineas liked that soft quality very very much.

Throughout the day, Phineas and Abigail hold hands. Over and over again, Phineas is asked to tell of the Great War. Phineas, however, is too humble a man to reply. With a shy smile, all he can say is, "I was sent over to bring music to those in despair and to remind them that love is the music of the heart. And that's what I tried to do."

Finally, the sun sets and the happy Heartlanders head for home.

Phineas and Abigail now find themselves alone. They stroll across the square to their home. Once inside, Phineas collapses onto the couch. Abigail curls up in his arms.

"To the day I die," Pepper says gently as he

strokes his wife's hair, "I promise to devote my life to making people happy!"

That's exactly what Sgt. Pepper did.

Old-timers will tell you there could never have been a Roaring Twenties without Sgt. Pepper's mad, merry, Charleston-playing band.

From midnight till dawn, they'd make music to dance the night away. On the lawn of the Heartland Hotel, beautiful flappers flapped and young beaus were never more dashing as they danced until the sun came up. Only then would the merriment finally stop. Everyone would collapse on the lawn, then rouse themselves at midday. And then they'd be ready to dance again.

And during the Great Depression, when Sgt. Pepper called those square dances, good times just had to be around the corner.

"Grab your partner and do-si-do. Alamand left and away we go!"

So poor they were dressed only in barrels, Heartlanders swung high and low, and none felt any pain. Oh, did they love that music! Oh, did that music wash away those grim Depression blues!

Who would have thought that economic recovery would have enabled Heartland to develop a society set? Who would have ever thought that Sgt. Pepper's Lonely Hearts Club Band would be playing at the Heartland Top Hat and Tails Society Cotillion Ball?

Pepper put down his baton and watched his friends and neighbors elegantly twirl their way around the floor. Every time a boy dipped a girl,

Phineas beamed ever so proudly. When Sgt. Pepper saw people in love, he knew he was making his dream come true.

Back to the trenches!

The second Great War! Pepper knew what had to be done!

On an airplane carrier in the South Pacific, just to the west of Bali, Pepper and his band, backed by none other than the great Glenn Miller, played and played. And when they thought they could play no more they introduced their guest stars, the one and only Andrews Sisters! My, did everyone's spirits soar!

Fighter planes stopped their shooting to listen to the music. Submarines emerged and swayed to the beat. Peace came suddenly to the raging sea.

August 16, 1956: How do you honor a man who has spent forty years making so many people so happy? Heartland thought long and hard, then decided to erect a Sgt. Pepper weathervane. This weathervane would always point the way to happiness!

Mr. Kite was to preside over the dedication ceremony. What an honor! After all, he had grown old along with Sgt. Pepper. Both men had known each other since boyhood. Now both were Senior Citizens—distinguished ones at that! Not only was Mr. Kite still Mayor, but Sgt. Pepper's Lonely Hearts Club Band—all in their late sixties and never out of touch with the times in which they lived—now played rock 'n' roll in the style of Bill Haley and The Comets and their great hit "Rock Around the Clock."

At ten o'clock that Saturday morning, all of Heartland lined the town square. They watched eagerly for noon.

Finally at the stroke of twelve, Mr. Kite proudly cut the ribbon. The gleaming weathervane was hoisted into the air. Suddenly, there it was on top of Heartland City Hall. From this vantage point, the weathervane could see all of Heartland, and all of Heartland could see it! The weathervane spun merrily around in the breeze.

The Heartlanders looked up and felt good. For all time, Sgt. Pepper would look after them . . . or so they thought. . . .

Mr. Kite turned toward the Heartland bandstand. He bowed in the direction of the heavily whiskered, beaming old veteran of two world wars.

Sgt. Pepper bowed back. He would repay his friends and neighbors for their lifelong love and devotion by playing rock 'n' roll as it had never been played before.

The first number had hardly begun when the Sergeant began to waver. He clutched his heart; he fell to his knees.

"Not our Sgt. Pepper!" gasped the crowd. They buried their faces in their hands. When they had gathered enough courage to look up, Sgt. Pepper lay on the ground, dead.

The next day at precisely the same time, the Heartlanders once again lined the town square. This time, however, there was tragedy instead of joy on their faces.

"I don't remember a time without Sgt. Pepper and his music," sighed one Heartland woman.

"It's as if a part of me has died," wept another.

A Heartland husband comforted his wife: "Don't

think that way, dear. Sgt. Pepper will live in our hearts forever!"

The casket containing Sgt. Pepper was placed on a horse-drawn hearse. The Heartlanders marched behind it as it was pulled up Heartland Hill to Heartland Cemetery.

They sobbed and moaned as the casket was lowered into the cold, hard ground. Then the Heartlanders slowly marched down the hill to their homes. They did not believe they could go on without Sgt. Pepper.

Mr. Kite grasped a friend's hand, then that friend clasped another's, until finally everyone in the town stood silently, hand in hand.

Mr. Kite looked up at the Sgt. Pepper weathervane as if in prayer and quietly said, "We will not let you down, Phineas. As Mayor of Heartland, I promise to see that all of us, as well as our children and the children of our children, practice kindness here and forever more."

Everyone bowed their heads in silent agreement.

Sgt. Pepper left a will. The first part of it was addressed to his beloved homeland!

To the town of Heartland—I leave the musical instruments played by the Lonely Hearts Club Band. These musical instruments have the power to make dreams come true. As long as they stay here, Heartland will always be a town of kindness and joy.

If they leave, who knows what evil dreams they might help other people fulfill?

If they leave, who knows what will happen to Heartland?

The Heartlanders promised they would protect the instruments with their lives. They did not want Heartland to turn mean like those cities and towns they read about in the daily newspapers and saw on the evening news.

There was more to Sgt. Pepper's will:

To my daughter, Saralinda, her husband, Ernest, and their mean-spirited stepson, Dougie Shears, I leave my house, barn and fields with instructions to keep them working.

Even though Dougie Shears was only seven, Sgt. Pepper had already realized that he was a bad egg.

Dougie was the son of Sgt. Pepper's son-in-law, Ernest, and Ernest's first wife, the high-spirited, fun-loving, frivolous Annabelle. Annabelle had lived only for fun! So one day she ran away from Heartland to join a girlie show and was never spoken of again.

Then Ernest met Saralinda. It was love at first sight. They were married just as the leaves began to turn gold and summer turned to autumn.

Saralinda loved Dougie Shears as if he were her own child. Eventually, Saralinda and Ernest had a son together—Billy. Even as a baby, Billy was something very special. His giggle was the most melodic anyone had ever heard. His smile was dazzling. The wisps of golden hair on his forehead literally glowed.

Though he was loved as much as Billy was, Dougie refused to let his wounds heal. Dougie was handsome and fair-haired, but his almost transparent blue eyes always revealed a profound suspicion of being alive. There was a piercing nervous

quality about him—a feeling of being trapped,
like some caged animal. When he was a mere four,
he too had run away!

"Just like his mother!" gasped the astonished
Heartlanders. They then observed that anybody
who runs away from happiness spends the rest
of his life with a black cloud over his head.

Indeed there was a black cloud over Dougie's
head—a full-time black cloud. Dougie hated everybody and everything.

He especially hated his step-brother, Billy. When
Billy was very small, Dougie would look right past
his step-brother and pretend he was invisible. No
matter how much Billy would plead, Dougie would
say, "I can hear you, but I can't see you! I'll never
see you!"

When Billy was nine, Dougie stole his mother's
grocery money from the cookie jar and blamed it
on Billy.

Dougie would also drop flies into his step-
brother's milk.

Billy tried to win Dougie's love by being even
kinder, but that only made Dougie's meanness
greater!

Yes, there was definitely a black cloud over
Dougie Shears' head.

There was another important clause in Sgt.
Pepper's will:

> *To my beloved grandson, Billy Shears, I
> leave my cherished Purple Staff.*

You could almost hear Sgt. Pepper's voice as
this next part of the will was read:

Grow up, Billy, and form a new Sgt. Pepper's Lonely Hearts Club Band! And in that Band, feature your three best friends, Mark, Dave and Bob Henderson! Billy, make music that always makes people happy! There is no finer work you can do!

The Purple Staff was slipped over young Billy's neck. The little boy looked toward the heavens. There was a determined look on his face. He had silently made a vow to fulfill his beloved grandfather's request. He would indeed grow up to form a new Sgt. Pepper's Lonely Hearts Club Band. That band would do the memory of his grandfather proud!

Young Mark, Dave and Bob Henderson had also loved Sgt. Pepper. They too vowed to make the late Sergeant's dream come true. They were Billy's best friends from the time they could walk and talk. They had begun to make music together in the Heartland Elementary School Glee Club. Every Christmas they would stroll from house to house, singing happy tunes: "Row, Row, Row Your Boat," "Georgie," "Dreidel, Dreidel," and "Baa-Baa, Black Sheep."

Everyone marveled at the fabled melting vocal harmonies they could create. They couldn't wait until that sound was part of a new Sgt. Pepper's Lonely Hearts Club Band.

For the generations to come, a Sgt. Pepper Museum was installed in Heartland City Hall. Mr. Kite was given the additional responsibility of being museum guard as well as Mayor.

Mr. Kite could not have been sweeter, more adorable or more proud. He was proud to have been Sgt. Pepper's best friend, proud to have been Mayor of Heartland for forty years, and proud to be in charge of the Museum in which resided the memory of the beloved Sergeant.

Mr. Kite loved to hold the hands of the Heartland tykes as he took them on tours of the Sgt. Pepper Museum. He would show them the walls covered with photographs of Sgt. Pepper's career, plus photographs of Sgt. Pepper with Presidents Woodrow Wilson, Warren G. Harding, Calvin Coolidge, Herbert C. Hoover, Franklin Delano Roosevelt, Harry S Truman and Dwight D. Eisenhower.

He would also show them Sgt. Pepper's first shoes (bronzed, of course), Sgt. Pepper's highchair, Sgt. Pepper's baby bib, Sgt. Pepper's toothbrushes, Sgt. Pepper's lunch box, Sgt. Pepper's Heartland High School yearbooks, as well as hundreds of letters, ribbons and certificates Sgt. Pepper had received from the world's great leaders.

Most impressive, however, was a life-sized floor-to-ceiling set of effigies of Sgt. Pepper's Lonely Hearts Club Band. As life-like as anything anyone had ever seen, their wrinkled eyes were filled with the widsom, as well as the joy, of the world; their stance was erect, as if they were leading the grandest of marches; their smiles revealed the pride that comes from only doing good.

These effigies were dressed in spectacular costumes. In the hands of each of them was one of Sgt. Pepper's cherished musical instruments. Each instrument was surrounded by its own aura, the color of pure gold.

Once again, the Heartlanders pressed Mr. Kite for the answers to certain questions:

Would Billy Shears grow up to form a new Sgt. Pepper's Lonely Hearts Club Band? And if there was a new Sgt. Pepper's Lonely Hearts Club Band, what, indeed, would that new band sound like?

"Be patient," said Mr. Kite. "In time! One day there'll be a new band. Just you wait and see!"

So they waited, and waited. . . .

TWO

Morning—Heartland, Today

It is dawn. The Heartland town square has already come alive with hustle and bustle. It's Fair Day, and Fair Day always means a flurry of last-minute preparations.

The brashy boys blow up hundreds of balloons.

The silly girls dress up their Kisses-for-Sale Booth with a coat of fresh pink paint.

The children practice for the bubble-gum-blowing competition.

In their homes, the women of Heartland iron their clothes, and the men polish their shoes.

Meanwhile the early comers set out blankets on the grass in front of the Heartland bandstand and lie back and soak up the warm sun.

Lovely Sylvia and Banker Tom spread their plaid blanket under a large maple tree.

"I want a large hunk of Farmer Chris's new cantaloupes." Tom's mouth waters.

"I'd like a slice of Norma's chocolate mousse pie and some fresh biscuits with Judy's homemade ginger preserves."

Tom is amazed. "You're going to eat all that?"

"Sure!" replies Sylvia.

Rena and her husband, Librarian Richard, have already found themselves a sunny spot and are looking over the stands.

Rena points. "Over there, Cheryl's quilts, the blue-and-yellow signature quilt, that's the one I want."

"If I win the weightlifting medal, you can have the quilt!"

"I know you'll win!" Rena trills happily. "I just know it!"

On the other side of the town square, Postman Hank's first stop is always the Heartland Confectionery Bakery, run by Norma and George Atkins. Norma pours Hank a cup of coffee and hands him a freshly baked turnover. She scans a postcard from her sister, Ruthie. The postcard makes her bubble with excitement. "Ruthie is coming to the fair," she announces. "She'll be here this afternoon! She couldn't have asked for a better day!"

Peter, a brashy boy, suddenly runs by the bakery shop window carrying a handful of green and blue helium balloons.

Mr. Kite, surrounded by a dozen adoring children, sits on the steps of Heartland City Hall.

"Do you remember last year's fair?" he reminisces. "Brash Peter was tired of trying to win silly Mimi a stuffed Teddy bear."

The children do not remember.

"Well," he continues, "anyway, Peter spent most of his allowance—and most of the afternoon—trying to win that Teddy bear. But Mark

Henderson just stepped up and with one single try won it. Mimi's been crazy about Mark ever since."

The sun climbs higher in the sky. The Heartlanders mop their brows as they stop to admire each other's achievements.

"That's a prize-winning bull you've got there," Butcher Jack tells Farmer Jasper. "I'm proud of you!"

"I've never seen such a huge watermelon," Teacher Ellen tells Farmer Chris.

"It's as juicy as it's big," Chris beams back. "Like a slice?"

Ellen smiles modestly at Chris. "I'd love one."

Meanwhile, the silly girls and the brashy boys play tag as they run around the stands. They dart from booth to booth, full of youthful fun and mischief.

"Mimi, slow down!" yells Peter. "This year I'm going to win you a prize."

"You'll have to win me first!" And off she goes. And off goes Peter after her.

Everywhere there's great expectation! The Heartland tots grow wilder and wilder with excitement. They whirl each other around until they are wildly dizzy. Giddily, they bump into each other. Then they fall down on the ground and laugh themselves silly.

It is noon, the official starting time of the Heartland Fair. The fair begins in slow motion. Couples stroll hand in hand around the square, first stopping to admire a display of fresh preserves, then moving on to the hand-sewn quilts. Ms. Claudia Johnson, Heartland's very own Grandma Moses, sits in front of her easel doing charcoal sketches of her friends and neighbors.

And Peter still pursues Mimi.

The momentum continues to build.

Peter can't find Mimi, but he does find some hot buttered corn.

Teacher Ellen leads her fourth-grade students on a tour of the Heartland flora and fauna exhibit.

Brashy Hans flips pizzas in the air as silly Carrie waits anxiously. She drools for the pizza—and she drools for Hans.

Brashy Jack suddenly grabs the pizza from her mouth, and she begins to chase him.

And then Dougie Shears mounts the Heartland bandstand. Everybody freezes in place. This is the moment Heartland has been waiting for.

Mark, Dave and Bob Henderson also take to the stage. Dressed in colorful shirts and snazzy jeans, they are as handsome as they are young—Heartland sons at their very best. The Hendersons pick up their instruments and begin to tune up. The crowd goes wild.

Behind them are the Heartland Old-Timers Swing and Jazz Ensemble: the liveliest old-timers ever to be found on the planet Earth. They are: eighty-seven-year-old Jerry Jones, who plays the meanest trumpet in town; eighty-three-year-old "Old Man" Al Francis on cornet; seventy-nine-year-old "Sly-as-a-Fox" Dandy Williams on trumpet; eighty-four-year-old "Fat Man" Dean on clarinet; and the kid of the group, "Sassy Sam," on flute—he's seventy-six if he's a day.

Dressed in red, white and blue ice-cream suits, the Heartland Old-Timers Swing and Jazz Ensemble has never looked snazzier. The crowd cheers them too.

Dougie taps the microphone. The silly girls scream in anticipation. The brashy boys jump up and down and whistle, and clap their hands over their heads.

The Sgt. Pepper weathervane has turned toward the bandstand. There is a smile of satisfaction on the weathervane's face.

Dougie holds up his hands for order. As manager of Sgt. Pepper's Lonely Hearts Club Band, he gets to make all the public announcements. He also is in charge of costumes, transportation and money. There are times when the boys are not quite sure they're getting their fair share, but on a day like today, who cares?

"Here they are!" Dougie shouts merrily. "On rhythm guitar, Mark Henderson!"

Mark steps forward. The silly girls wave frantically to him from the crowd.

Mark smiles and waves back. Darkly handsome, he is the kind of romantic idol who got all the valentines in elementary school—and still does.

Continues Dougie, "Now say hello to our drummer, Dave Henderson!"

Dave stands up behind his drum kit and waves at the silly girls who waved at Mark. The silly girls giggle. They always giggle when they see Dave. They giggle because there is always a sly look in Dave's eyes, a sign of mischief. This boy is always having mischief-filled thoughts.

"And now, on keyboards, here's Bob Henderson."

Bob runs up and squirts the crowd with a water pistol. They all laugh. Bob is a clown, a cut-up who likes the girls, but would rather keep them laughing.

Their laughing turns to cheers the minute the music starts.

Dougie begins to sing. Then Mark, Dave and Bob join in.

It was twenty years ago today that
Sergeant Pepper taught the band
   to play
They've been going in and out of
   style
But they're guaranteed to raise
   a smile
So may I introduce to you
The act you've known for all
   these years
*Sergeant Pepper's Lonely Hearts
   Club Band*

We're Sergeant Pepper's Lonely
   Hearts Club Band
We hope you will enjoy the show
We're Sergeant Pepper's Lonely
   Hearts Club Band
Sit back and let the evening go
Sergeant Pepper's Lonely
Sergeant Pepper's Lonely
Sergeant Pepper's Lonely Hearts
   Club Band

It's wonderful to be here
It's certainly a thrill
You're such a lovely audience
We'd like to take you home with us,
We'd love to take you home

I don't really want to stop
   the show

But I thought you might like
to know

That the singer is going to
sing a song
And he wants you all to sing
along
So may I introduce to you
The one and only *Billy Shears.*
And *Sergeant Pepper's Lonely
Hearts Club Band!!!*

The crowd cannot contain its excitement. Billy runs through the audience. As he passes by, the Heartlanders scream. "We love you, Billy!" "Billy, you're so terrific, I can't stand it!" "You're so beautiful!" "Billy, sing to me—only to me!"

Billy jumps onto the stage. The applause is deafening.

The Sgt. Pepper weathervane swells with pride. No grandfather could have ever hoped for a better grandson.

Billy is a wonderfully radiant young man with long golden hair and Sgt. Pepper's emerald-green eyes. He proudly wears Sgt. Pepper's Purple Staff around his neck. It honors him to make Sgt. Pepper's dream come true.

Mark, Dave and Bob slap Billy on the back. Then Bob squirts Billy in the face with his water pistol. Billy, in return, pulls Bob's hat over Bob's eyes.

The crowd eats it up and yells for more.

Billy flashes his bright smile. "One-two, one-two-three!" he calls. Then he begins to sing and play.

What would you do if I sang out
   of tune
Would you stand up and walk out
   on me?
Lend me your ears and I'll sing
   you a song
And I'll try not to sing out of
   key
Oh, I get by with a little help from
   my friends
Mm, I get high with a little help
   from my friends.
Mm, I'm gonna try with a little help
   from my friends.
What do I do when my love is away?
(Does it worry you to be alone?)
How do I feel by the end of the
   day?
(Are you sad because you're on
   your own?)
No, I get by with a little help
   from my friends
Mm, I get high with a little help
   from my friends.
Going to try with a little help from
   my friends.

Do you need anybody?
I need somebody to love.
Could it be anybody?
I want somebody to love.
Would you believe in a love at
   first sight?
Yes, I'm certain it happens all
   the time.

(What do you see when you turn
   out the light?)
I can't tell you but I know it's
   mine.
Oh, I get by with a little help from
   my friends.
Mm, I get high with a little help
   from my friends.
Going to try with a little help from
   my friends.

Do you need anybody?
I just need someone to love.
Could it be anybody?
I want somebody to love.
Oh, I get by with a little help from
   my friends
Mm, I'm gonna try with a little help
   from my friends.
Oh, I get high with a little
   help from my friends
With a little help from my friends.
With a little help from my friends.

The energy that emerges from this music instantly makes everyone's feet tap, fingers snap, and body sway. This music makes you feel good! It makes you glad to be alive!

Mr. Kite sits on a rocking chair on the front porch of Heartland City Hall. He taps his toes and smiles delightedly to himself. This band is all that the original Sgt. Pepper's Lonely Hearts Club Band ever was! he thinks to himself. A miracle has come true!

The crowd boogies in front of the bandstand. The brashy boys and the silly girls leap high into the air! When the band sings of love, the audience shouts back, "We love you!" And they do! No music has ever made them so happy, has ever made them want to dance and sing, has ever made them feel that every single day will be sunny from this day on.

"I love you! We love you!" Their shouts fill the air.

Strawberry Fields watches happily from the porch of Heartland's Home for Our Beloved Aged. She is proud to be Billy Shears' girl friend. Radiantly beautiful, her blonde hair looks as if it had been rinsed by sunlight. She and Billy have loved each other since they were small children. She can remember as far back as when they were both only five. All the Heartland kids were in the Heartland Park on a naturally beautiful Sunday afternoon. Strawberry was pushing her doll carriage, and Billy was racing the Henderson brothers on his tricycle. He was going so fast that his feet got tangled up in the pedals and he lost control. He ran right into Strawberry, knocking down both her and her carriage.

Billy helped her up. "Gee, I'm really sorry. I hurt myself, too. See?" And he showed her a bloody knee.

"You better wash that right away."

"Okay, but when I get back, can I give you a ride on my tricycle? I'll drive it more slowly."

Strawberry nodded "yes." She was in love.

Strawberry is a student nurse now at the Heartland Home for Our Beloved Aged, which is run by her parents, Linda and Stuart Fields. She works there; her family lives in a small apartment on the Heartland's Home's second floor.

Linda and Stuart Fields are an extremely proper-looking, middle-aged pair, too conservative to be pleased that their only daughter loves a musician. But they respect her enough to trust her judgment. And anyway, Billy is such a good boy!

Strawberry looks lovingly at her boyfriend on the bandstand. Last night, after his rehearsal, they had plopped down on the bandstand to stare up at the stars above. The stars had twinkled at each other as if they were in intimate conversation. There were so many stars out that Billy said it looked like a convention of angels. The moon grew brighter and larger. Finally, it got very late.

It became time to go.

Billy did not want the evening to end. "Let's play a game," he said.

"What game?" Strawberry did not want to leave either.

"It's called 'My Favorite Time.' "

"I've never heard of it."

"I ask you a question and you answer it. For instance, 'What was your favorite school dance?' "

Strawberry closes her eyes and thinks. "Let's see, there were so many. . . . Maybe the one where you became so jealous of Sam that you dumped the bowl of punch over his head." The memory makes her laugh.

She looks at Billy. "Now I get to ask a question." Strawberry is having fun. "Which was your favorite baseball game?"

"You mean a game that I played in?"

"Yes."

"Probably the last one that I won!" Billy suddenly has another thought. "Do you remember the game when Dougie sold twice as many tickets as there were seats?" They both laugh. "That was my favorite!"

"And when he was caught," remembers Strawberry, "his punishment was to clean all the bleacher seats!"

They are both quiet for a minute. The heavens are wondrously bright. "Strawberry," Billy asks quietly, "what's the softest thing you ever touched?"

Strawberry thinks. "I guess Tilly, our goose, is pretty soft, or Ivy's Persian cat. . . . No, I know—Farmer Morgan's newborn chicks. I couldn't believe how soft they were when I held them to my face. . . . What's the softest thing you've ever touched?"

"You are."

The answer moves Strawberry.

"You have the softest skin. Sometimes when I touch you, I'm almost afraid you'll melt away. . . ."

Strawberry turns away. Billy puts his arm protectively around her shoulders. They gaze warmly into each other's eyes.

Strawberry can see those eyes before her now as she looks out at the happy crowd.

Then her memory flashes back to a spring afternoon when she and Billy had been walking hand in hand. They had been talking for hours about anything and everything. They never seemed to run out of things to share.

Strawberry had bent down to pick some flowers. "Do you know the thing I like best about you?"

Billy was curious. "No. What?"

"You're always exciting!"

Billy had looked puzzled.

"No matter whether we're dancing, whether you're helping me at work, or whether we're just doing homework together, just being with you is exciting!"

Billy is pleased. He had never thought of himself as being "exciting" before. "Do you know what I like best about you?"

"What?"

"I like the way you touch things. When you touch something, you make it beautiful! Remember those broken dolls we found in the garage? It took you only ten minutes to mend them, and then their smiles suddenly grew bigger! They really did!"

Strawberry had run through the field blowing on dandelions and laughing as the dandelion fuzz had scattered into the air. Billy had run after her. When he had caught up, he had taken her hand and pulled her toward him.

"You make my heart beat so fast."

Then Strawberry had lightly kissed his forehead, his eyelids, his nose, and the corners of his mouth. She had gently kissed his neck.

"Strawberry, you're standing in Mrs. Vincent's way. She can't see the band!" Mrs. Fields speaks sharply enough to shatter the daydream.

Strawberry steps behind Mrs. Vincent's wheelchair. She gently pushes it from the porch toward the band. Mrs. Vincent is delighted. "We love you, Billy!" she calls merrily.

Strawberry laughs along with Mrs. Vincent.

There isn't an old person in Heartland who doesn't love music, fun, and excitement. And everyone loves the old folks. After all, they're the lucky ones who have lived longer than anybody else in this wonderful town. They love being alive, and every day just gets better and better. These old folks have lived to see both the original Sgt. Pepper's Lonely Hearts Club Band and this *new* Lonely Hearts Club Band—this band that makes them boogie all day long. Suddenly they can't sit still. All they want to do is dance, dance, dance.

Billy is in the midst of a love song. He sees Strawberry coming. He directs the song toward her. Their eyes meet; signals of love flash back and forth.

In front of the bandstand, Dougie hawks pictures of the band. He spots Strawberry, pushes through the crowd, then reaches out and playfully spins her around.

Strawberry pushes him away. She continues eagerly toward Billy.

Dougie is stunned. He hates rejection. Billy Shears has the prettiest girl in town, and he has nobody. He chases after Strawberry and blocks her path.

"Dougie, later! I have to see Billy now!"

But Dougie won't let her pass.

Dougie has always been jealous of Billy's relationship with Strawberry. He had tried to woo Strawberry by bringing her bouquets of spring flowers; he ordered imported presents for her from mail-order catalogues; he had the Elementary School Glee Club serenade her; but she never paid any attention. She loved only Billy, and that was that!

Suddenly the crowd's attention is diverted as a loud beep is heard above the music. All eyes turn toward Messenger Charlie. Charlie is the world's oldest Western Union Messenger; he has a certificate to prove it! He is ninety-seven if he's a day! He bicycles his way toward the bandstand.

"Telegram for the Lonely Hearts Club Band," he announces upon reaching his destination.

The music stops. Everyone is stunned. Who would be sending the band a telegram? There had not been a telegram sent to a Heartlander in four-teen years. Then, Norma's sister, Ruthie, had sent a wire from London stating that she was coming for a visit. Once before that, Billie Holiday had sent a wire announcing that she would sing with Sgt. Pepper's Lonely Hearts Club Band on July 4 at the Heartland Fair. But that was that!

Billy reaches down and clutches the telegram. He rips it open and reads it to the crowd:

> BIG DEAL RECORDS, THE WORLD'S LARGEST, MOST SUCCESSFUL RECORD COMPANY, HAS LEARNED THAT YOUR MUSIC IS GREAT. WE NEED A TAPE OF YOUR SONGS! WE NEED IT NOW! SEND TAPE IMMEDIATELY TO OUR L.A. OFFICE. IF WE LIKE YOUR MUSIC, WE WILL MAKE YOU SUPERSTARS!
>
> SIGNED, B.D. BROCKHURST, PRESIDENT, BIG DEAL RECORDS

There was the time that the *Heartland Gazette* had published little Heather's poem. What an exciting moment that had been in the history of Heartland!

Then there was the day Ellen and Chris danced nonstop for twenty-seven hours and won the Heartland Marathon. Another Heartland thriller-diller!

But a telegram from Los Angeles saying that you could become a *superstar!* This was the most overwhelming thing that had ever happened to any Heartlander. Everyone was rendered speechless.

A wide-eyed Mark looks at Bob; a wide-eyed Bob looks at Dave; a wide-eyed Dave looks at

Mark; a wide-eyed Lonely Hearts Club Band looks at Billy; a wide-eyed Billy looks back at them. Astonishment reigns supreme!

Then Billy begins to regain his senses. He reaches down, pulls Strawberry onto the stage and kisses her impulsively. The boys all kiss Strawberry. She kisses them.

Suddenly everyone hugs and kisses each other! How else do you celebrate the most exciting day in the history of Heartland?

The boys wave the telegram above their heads; they play leapfrog on each other's shoulders. They could be superstars!

Silly Mimi, silly Carrie and silly Dodie jump onto the stage. They hug Mark wildly. They are jubilant!

"Mark, you're going to be famous!" Carrie squeals.

Mimi wraps herself around Mark's knees. "Take me to Hollywood with you. I want to be famous also!"

Mark, however, hears not a word of it. He is long gone in his own personal daydream. There he is in Hollywood, zooming down the freeway in the world's most expensive super sports car! Eight of the world's most beautiful women are packed into the tiny vehicle beside him. They caress him, blow in his ear, toy with locks of his hair. . . .

Dodie, the most giggly of the silly girls, throws her arms around Bob. "Bobby, you're going to be rich!"

"Rich!" Bob is lost in his own dream. He is riding through Hollywood in a chauffeur-driven limousine packed with floor-to-ceiling-high stacks of money. The street is lined with thousands of loyal fans. He opens the window and tosses the money into the air. He is so rich that the only thing left for him to do is give the money away. No wonder every time he appears there's dancing in the streets!

Dave smiles nonchalantly at the three silly girls flocked around Mark. He too has a dream. He too will be driven through town in a chauffeur-driven car. And Mark will be the driver!

Dougie says nothing. He just wants to get to Los Angeles as fast as he can. He wants to escape from a world in which no matter what he does he can never win.

The Heartlanders hoist the boys onto their shoulders; they are marched around the town square just as Sgt. Pepper had been when he had returned from both Great Wars.

The Sgt. Pepper weathervane spins happily in the breeze. And somewhere in heaven, Sgt. Pepper is happy too. The Lonely Hearts Club Band has done exactly what he asked in his will. They made music "that always made people happy!" Now they will set out to share their music with the world! Soon the whole world will be dancing!

The sun begins to set—the official end of Heartland Fair Day. A comfortable quiet soothes the Heartlanders as they pack up their belongings.

Tired, but as giggly as ever, the silly girls walk home hand in hand with the brashy boys. The girls rest their heads quietly on the boys' shoulders.

Farmer Chris and Teacher Ellen share one more slice of watermelon together. Then they too clasp hands and stroll into the night.

Lovely Sylvia and Banker Tom fold their blanket. As their hands meet, they smile.

Rena and Librarian Richard gather their children around them as they watch the vivid orange-tinted sunset.

George and Norma have a final cup of coffee. Then George bends over and gently kisses Norma's nose. They give each other a gentle hug before they turn off the bakery light and head for home.

On the porch of the Heartland Home for Our Beloved Aged, the old men serenade the old women with their harmonicas. The old women gently run their hands through the old men's hair.

Billy and Strawberry sit on the Heartland bandstand. They watch the sun go down. Billy holds his breath until his face turns beefy-red.

"Billy, stop that!" exclaims Strawberry.

Billy holds his breath even harder.

"Why are you doing that?"

There is no response.

Strawberry gives Billy a gentle but firm poke in his stomach. Billy exhales dramatically. "No fair!"

"Why were you holding your breath?"

"I was afraid that if I started to breathe again, I'd discover that I'd been dreaming."

"It does seem like a dream."

Billy rests his hand on Strawberry's shoulder. "What do you think?" he asks anxiously.

"Billy, it's what you've aways worked for"— Strawberry turns away—"but I'll miss you. There's no denying that!"

The thought of leaving Strawberry has never entered Billy's mind until this very moment. It makes him sad. Billy and Strawberry look into each other's eyes. Then Billy grabs Strawberry and hugs her hard.

The Lonely Hearts Club Band equipment truck turns the corner.

"Let's go!" Dougie shouts to Billy. He can't bear to see them together.

"I'll see you after dinner." Billy gives Strawberry a good-bye kiss and then dashes to the truck. The truck drives past Heartland City Hall. Mr. Kite sits on the porch puffing a cigar and watching night descend. The boys wave to him; he waves back.

Billy turns and watches Strawberry walking slowly toward the Heartland Home for Our Beloved Aged.

Mark, Dave and Bob give Billy a series of friendly whacks on the back.

"We're going to make it!" announces Dave. "We've got Sgt. Pepper on our side!"

Bob steps on the gas and the pick-up truck zooms off into the night.

Mr. Kite watches the truck pull away. There is an elfish grin on his face. Slowly, he trods from City Hall across the grass to the bandstand. Somewhat short of breath, he sits down on it and lights up another cigar.

Bobbie and Bonnie, two ponytailed little girls who love Mr. Kite and whom Mr. Kite loves with equal affection, have been eyeing the Mayor from a distance. They can't wait any longer. They dash toward the bandstand. "Mr. Kite, please tell us a story."

But Mr. Kite doesn't feel like storytelling. There is a time of the day when everyone should be allowed to let his imagination run wild. Sunset is Mr. Kite's time of day. And now he fantasizes that he too is a superstar, just like the one Billy Shears is about to become.

Mr. Kite stands center stage on the bandstand.

Even though he has arthritis, rheumatism and gout, he suddenly feels young. In his mind's eye, he is dressed in jeans and an open shirt and there's a guitar slung around his neck. Mr. Kite takes the hands of Bobbie and Bonnie and pulls them into his dream.

"Girls, can't you see the crowd out there screaming for the new rock sensation? They don't want Mick Jagger; they don't want Rod Stewart. They want me!"

Bobbie stands in the middle of the bandstand. "Ladies and gentlemen, let me introduce you to the one, the only, America's newest rock 'n' roll sensation, Heartland's answer to Led Zeppelin, The Eagles and Fleetwood Mac—Mr. Kite!"

Mr. Kite begins to sing one of the Lonely Hearts Club Band's most enticing compositions:

> I'm fixing a hole where the
>   rain gets in
> And stops my mind from wandering
> Where it will go.
> I'm filling the cracks that ran
>   through the door
> And kept my mind from wandering
> Where it will go.
>
> And it doesn't really matter if
> I'm wrong I'm right
> Where I belong I'm right
> Where I belong
> See the people standing there who
>   disagree and never win
> And wonder why they don't get in
>   my door

I'm painting the room in a
     colorful way
And when my mind is wandering
There I will go
And it really doesn't matter if
I'm wrong I'm right
Where I belong I'm right
Where I belong

Silly people run around they
     worry me
And never ask me why they don't
     get past my door
I'm taking my time for a number
     of things
That weren't important yesterday
And I still go
I'm fixing a hole where the rain
     gets in
And stops my mind from wandering
Where it will go.

Mr. Kite signals Bonnie. "A drum roll, please."
Bonnie pantomimes a roll of the drums.

"Girls, how about a little soft shoe? Follow me."

The sun is setting over Heartland, and on the Heartland bandstand one old gentleman and two little girls are tapping their hearts out.

Mr. Kite suddenly returns to his dream of rock 'n' roll superstardom. "No, no, girls," he announces. "No more concert dates! No more covers of *Rolling Stone!* No more groupies asking for my autograph! No more of anything! I've had enough!"

Bonnie gets down on one knee. "Oh, please, Mayor, baby, one more song! Just give us one more tune for old times' sake!"

"Please, please!" pleads Bobbie. "You owe it to your public!"

"Ah, my public!" Once again, Mr. Kite takes the hands of the little girls. They dance down the bandstand and around the town square. They dance the Splash, the Monkey, the Frug, the Boog-a-loo, the Latin Tango, the Freak and the New York Hustle. Then they make pirouettes and play leapfrog. And then they tap again. Every night at sunset Mr. Kite is truly young.

Dinner is finished and the boys have gone about their business. Ernest finishes a piece of Norma's chocolate mousse pie, but Saralinda can't touch a bite.

Ernest and Saralinda Shears sit quietly at the dining room table. Ernest does his best to comfort his grieving wife. "I'm not worried about this trip to Los Angeles," he says with as much heartiness as he can muster. "Dougie has good business sense, and nobody is a better human being than Billy."

"But Los Angeles?" gasps Saralinda. "What if there's an earthquake? And they've got motels that show naughty movies! These boys have never been out of Heartland!"

Ernest laughs. "Dougie is already corrupt! And Billy is decent enough to reform a couple of sinners."

"You're taking this all too easily!" replies Mrs. Shears. "Nothing good ever happened to anybody who ever left Heartland!"

Ernest says nothing. History has shown indeed that his wife is quite right.

Dougie paces back and forth in front of the barn. He is a dreamer who dreams big! He sees the band performing in an arena holding millions of fans, all throwing money wildly at the stage. Dougie is there with a broom, sweeping, sweeping, sweeping. Thousands scream adoringly at him.

It's bedtime. Zena Henderson rubs night cream on her face. Ever since B.D. Brockhurst's telegram arrived, she has been brooding about Mark, Dave and Bob leaving home.

Bill Henderson is doing the last of his fifty sit-ups. ". . . forty-six, forty-seven, forty-eight . . ."

"What about the floods?" she says suddenly. "Los Angeles has hideous floods."

Bill Henderson is equally nervous. "Floods?" he replies. "Who's worried about floods? Have you considered drugs? They don't eat dinner in Los Angeles—they smoke it!"

Bill and Zena Henderson hold each other tightly. They are as scared as scared can be. What if the tape the boys make is as good as that record company in Los Angeles thinks it will be?

Bill and Zena Henderson have trained their sons to be independent young men. Now their sons just might do as they've been taught and leave their safe and secure home!

The Hendersons spend the night tossing back and forth wondering what will become of their sons if they choose to leave Heartland. There are so many possibilities and all of them are bad!

THREE

Throughout the entire next day Heartland was bubbling with excitement. Everyone hustled about, anxious to finish their day's work so they could run down to the barn and watch the Lonely Hearts Club Band make their tape for Big Deal Records.

Samantha closed the café for dinner. Norma and Baker George packed pastries to bring to the taping. The silly girls spent hours fixing their hair, and the brashy boys spent hours primping for the silly girls. The brashy boys know that this taping will make the Henderson boys even more desirable to the girls. "Drat!" they said as each of them combed his hair in a million different ways.

At sundown, Billy, Mark, Dave and Bob gather in the Shears' barn to make the tape. They rehearse a soft romantic number. A small group of Heartlanders sits on Heartland Bridge facing the barn. They hold hands and sway back and forth in time to the music. The Heartlanders sigh. No one writes and plays love songs like Sgt. Pepper's Lonely Hearts Club Band!

The band runs through the number again. Dougie does his best to capture the rich, melodic sound on his weatherworn tape recorder.

A ripe, glowing moon rises over Heartland. Brashy Jack has picked a handful of flowers. He hands them to Ivy and she smells them appreciatively. Farmer Chris and Teacher Ellen dangle their feet in Heartland Pond. Sometimes their feet touch. When they do, they giggle affectionately.

Sylvia has once again caught the eye of Banker Tom. He offers to share his apple cider with her. They take alternate sips. Suddenly they're in love!

Bob and Louis chase Laurie and Heather. At the Heartland Home for Our Beloved Aged, Big Ma Pearl hums a song of romance in the ear of Big Pa Marty.

Male ducks quack their mating call; female ducks quickly come flapping around. Pairs of chickens cluck a happy tune; pairs of geese do the same. Even the fireflies fly in pairs.

There are couples everywhere—all falling in love to the music made by Sgt. Pepper's Lonely Hearts Club Band.

The band takes a break in order to make some chord changes.

"Do you think they'll really move to Hollywood?" swoons Carrie.

The very notion of their leaving makes Mimi upset. "They'd never leave Heartland!" she says with finality.

"They'll leave, all right," teases Peter. "And the sooner the better, as far as I'm concerned."

"You're all wet!" squeals Carrie. She and Mimi turn and push Peter off the bridge into the pond.

The ducks honk furiously as Peter lands with a splash.

"Quiet out there!" barks Dougie. "We're ready to tape again."

Waves of reverberation suddenly come from Dave's beat-up amplifier. Dougie rushes over. He twists one dial; Dave twists another. Dougie pushes Dave's hands away, but Dave will have none of it. He furiously turns as many knobs as he can get his hands on. He will make this thing work at any cost!

Dougie once again pulls Dave's hands away.

Both Dougie and Dave vigorously turn knobs and push buttons. Horrible noises pour forth from the machine; then smoke starts to rise.

"Fire! Fire!" yells Bob.

The Heartlanders jump into the pond. Peter splashes each of them as they land. Soon all of Heartland Pond has been transformed into a huge water fight.

In the midst of the splashing and screaming, Billy quietly pulls the plug from the wall. "Folks, there's no fire," he says gently, and he begins to fix the amplifier.

Everyone in the pond looks sheepishly at each other. Soaked up to their necks, they've never had more fun, and they don't want that fun to end.

Strawberry sits quietly on a block of hay in the corner of the barn. She smiles at Billy; he smiles back.

Why doesn't Strawberry smile at him? Dougie wonders. Why does everyone always like Billy? Why do so few people like him? Dougie's face is cast in a permanent scowl.

The brashy boys are beginning to bore the silly girls. They now fuss and fret over Mark. He's the most beautiful boy they've ever seen. They bask in his radiance.

Carrie combs Mark's hair. "I think I'd like your bangs pushed forward," she declares.

Mimi primps Mark's shirt. "No, take his hair off his forehead so you can see those melting eyes of his." Mimi pushes back his hair. Accidentally, she steps on Dodie's fingers. Dodie has been shining the musician's shoes.

Dodie gives Mimi a shove. Mimi playfully pushes her back.

Meanwhile, Carrie has to put in her two cents. "Dodie, you haven't finished Mark's shoes!" she scolds. Carrie just loves to tease Dodie.

Dodie stops smacking Mimi and shoots a darting glance at Carrie. "Finish them yourself!" She throws a glob of shoe polish at Carrie. A direct hit! Carrie just easily smears polish all over Dodie's dress.

Mark steps back and watches. The shoe-polish fight is now in full gear and it makes him laugh. The boys whistle and yell as they urge on the warring girls from their vantage point in the pond. Then they return to their splashing.

The noise infuriates Dougie. Why can't this tape get made right? he wonders. This is the tape that could get him to Los Angeles, where he will become rich and powerful and never again have to play second fiddle to Billy.

"Girls, cut it out!" he screams. "We've got work to do—work that will take us out of here to the Big Time and away from you!"

The girls are tired of being put down by Dougie Shears. They jump on him, wrestle him to the ground, then give him an intense dose of the tickle torture. Dougie doesn't want to laugh—he never laughs—but he can't help himself now!

"Stop it! Stop it!" he screams as the girls relentlessly torment him.

"The amplifier is repaired," Billy suddenly announces. "Girls, we've got to finish this tape."

The girls stop immediately. Billy's recording session, after all, is the most important thing that has ever happened to Heartland.

The girls sit beside Strawberry. They share knowing smiles. All the girls had been in love with Billy when they were younger, but Billy never had eyes for anyone else but Strawberry.

The girls had tried to win his affection. At twelve, Mimi had given Strawberry a black eye so that Strawberry couldn't go to the school dance, but Billy spent that night looking after Strawberry at the Heartland Home for Our Beloved Aged. He would never go to a dance without her.

Carrie had worked at the soda fountain in Samantha's café during junior high school and had always given Billy an enormously large banana split. But Billy always shared it with Strawberry.

Dodie tied a hundred yellow ribbons to the old oak tree in front of the Shears' barn. But Billy had taken them down and given them to Strawberry.

It was a losing game, and the girls eventually had diverted their attention to the Henderson brothers.

Dougie glares at the girls as he heads for the equipment. The angry look in his eyes makes them break into peals of laughter.

Mimi nudges Strawberry. "Don't you think Mark has the sexiest eyes?"

Strawberry smiles.

Carrie gets in her two cents. "Oh, but it's his teeth. Have you ever seen such straight, white teeth?"

Dodie laughs. "Teeth? Are you nuts? Who cares about teeth? It's his walk, so sure and confident."

Strawberry casually observes, "I think his hair is awfully nice also."

All the girls yell together, "Oh no you don't! He's mine! You've got Billy!"

The thought of it makes Strawberry feel warm all over.

"All right, boys," says Billy. "From the top. One-two, one-two-three . . ."

The amplifier works; the tape recorder works. The recording session has finally begun.

The boys merrily begin to sing:

> It's getting better all the time
> I used to get mad at my school
> The teachers that taught me
>   weren't cool
> You're holding me down, turning
>   me 'round
> Filling me up with your rules
>
> I've got to admit it's getting
>   better
> A little better all the time
> I have to admit it's getting
>   better
> It's getting better since you've
>   been mine.
>
> Me used to be an angry young man
> Me hiding me head in the sand

You gave me the word
I finally heard
I'm doing the best that I can.

I've got to admit it's getting
    better
I used to be cruel to my woman
I beat her and kept her apart
    from the things that she loves
Man, I was mean but I'm changing
    my scene
And I'm doing the best that I can.

Yes, I admit it's getting better
It's getting better since you've
    been mine.
I admit it's getting better
A little better all the time

A nondescript mustard-colored van climbs to the top of Heartland Hill. It proceeds slowly, one wheel at a time, from side to side, like a cat stalking its prey. On its side are stenciled the words MUSTARD REAL ESTATE. The van continues its climb, belching yellow exhaust fumes all the while. With each belch, it makes an eerie moan of delight. How much fun it is to pollute such a clean, clean landscape!

Eagerly the van belches even more contamination into the atmosphere.

Then a periscope rises from the top of the van. It turns right, then left. Mr. Mustard checks out the terrain.

He loves what he sees! What a lovely place for the Mustard Industrial Park, the Mustard Shopping Center, the Mustard high-rise apartment complex, the Mustard slum, and especially Mr. Mustard's Greasy Mustard Burger Stand.

Mustard munches on a hot dog drenched with mustard. He wipes the mustard drippings onto the sleeve of his mustard-colored jacket. Yummy! Yummy! He loves his mustard because it's the color of jaundice.

Once he was a loser, this jowly toad thinks to himself. Once—but no more! Still, he cannot help musing about his early, loser days. Then, even his mother had no use for him.

"Loser, get away from me!" she'd bark as he drooled down the front of her dress.

And what a loser he'd been! After all, he had studied the accordion, invested in the Edsel, and voted for Richard M. Nixon—both times!

He had also tried to give his heart in love, and time after time he had been heartlessly rejected. Was it his bad breath, his dandruff, his stooped shoulders, his ill-fitting clothes, his inability to make small talk?—or was it all of these? He knew that he had grown to late-middle-age alone and loveless because all losers ever got was scorn. But now he was about to win. Heartland would be his!

He even had a team to help: Irma, Barbra and Martha. Made of transistors, nuts and bolts, with light-bulb eyes, wire spring hair and amplifier mouths, they were the most adorable computerettes he had ever seen.

These computer cuties had been assembled out of nuts and bolts right before Mustard's eyes. "Hey, you jerk!" they shouted from their amplifier mouths. "If you tighten that bolt anymore, we'll be AC-DC!" "Touch that wire one more time, buddy, and we'll permanently disconnect you!" "Hey, good-looking, turn that knob a little more to the right!"

Mustard had brought them home to his sleazy van. They all instantly adored him.

Barbra was determined to become Mrs. Mustard. A schemer, she would flirt with him day and night.

Rubbing his shoulders, she would scratch him behind the ears. "How does that feel, tiger?"

Martha would treat him like a mother. "Now, if you don't finish your supper, you'll never be strong enough to be a winner!"

And Irma, well, she truly had a crush on the old fool, and she would plot endlessly to get him away from Barbra. Not as bright as the others, few of Irma's schemes would work.

Martha's hair suddenly lights up. "Mustard, honey, Central Headquarters is sending us a message," she squeals.

All eyes focus on the huge videoscreen on the truck's back wall. After all, a message from Central Headquarters is always a privilege. Central Headquarters is where "FVB" lives!

Before "FVB" had chosen Mr. Mustard, Mustard had nothing. Now, because of "FVB," he had three singing computerettes and soon would have the town of Heartland, where he would be king! And "FVB" had also promised that he would finally get a girl—any girl he wanted!

Mustard knew that someday he would know what "FVB" stood for. But meanwhile, he would do whatever "FVB" bid. That's why he stares raptly at the videoscreen.

The message appears on the screen. It is the slogan of the Movement—time once again to pledge one's loyalty, something that happens three times daily.

WE HATE LOVE.

WE HATE JOY.

WE LOVE MONEY.

REMEMBER, LOSERS CAN BE WINNERS!

The four of them jump up and down. It's a dream come true! By the time they're done, this slogan will be more popular than "Plop, plop, fizz, fizz, oh what a relief it is!"

Their spirits are so high that they dance around the van. Suddenly, it lurches to a screaming halt. Mr. Mustard and his computer cuties land on the floor. He is not pleased.

"Dummy, why have we stopped?" he screams to his driver, Brute.

There is no answer.

Mr. Mustard throws open the door that separates the living quarters from the cab of the van. Brute's enormous square head with its two basset-hound eyes nods dopily in time to the lilting music made by the Lonely Hearts Club Band.

Mustard glowers. He presses a button on the dashboard. A boxer's glove pops out and punches Brute square in the face. Brute is a happy man.

Poor Brute! At his first battle, this eight-foot giant looked like a promising prizefighter—until his opponent started humming "Melancholy Baby" in the third round. Brute—always a sucker for romantic music! He looked adoringly at his opponent, and he was instantly knocked out!

After that, it was all downhill, until at the bottom rung of the ladder Mr. Mustard appointed him his chauffeur-bodyguard.

Still, whenever the air is filled with melody, Brute can't help drifting off into a world of mists and dancing nymphs. Guitar solos especially set him flying, and this band certainly does have a terrific guitar player.

Mustard steps back into the living quarters of the van. The computerettes are at the periscope. As they turn it, close-ups of Heartland appear on the videoscreen.

Mustard carefully surveys the town he will soon take over. Teacher Ellen is leading her students through the fields on a nature-study walk. Her dog, Sasha, runs side by side with them.

Samantha serves lunch outside on the bandstand to Postman Hank. She knows that Hank works very hard and deserves to be catered to.

Mr. Kite sits on the porch of the Heartland Museum and tells a story to Heather and Laurie.

Banker Tom escorts lovely Sylvia down to Cheryl's to help pick out new drapes for her lovely bedroom. They stop for a moment and give each other a loving hug.

Then the Shears' barn pops up. Irma switches on the X-ray scanner; now Mustard can see inside the barn. There is a close-up of the Lonely Hearts Club Band making the music that is driving Brute mad. And then Mustard spots Strawberry Fields!

"Stop!" he screams. "Stop!"

Now the entire screen is taken up by Strawberry.

Mr. Mustard drools uncontrollably. So sweet! So naïve! So ripe! Mustard smacks his lips. He moans as he pushes the computerettes away and jiggles the periscope himself to ensure the best view. "I must make her mine!" he says over and over again. No woman had ever been so pure. Like sugar! He would truly be a winner if he could capture this beauty's heart. Yes, he would have her, one way or another. . . .

Irma has turned red with rage. She grabs the periscope and spins it around until it belts Mr. Mustard in the eye.

"Hey, hot lips," scheming Barbra suddenly chortles, "there's another message coming in."

Still dreaming of Strawberry, Mr. Mustard turns back to the screen:

> KEEP YOUR MIND ON BUSINESS.
> TAKE OVER HEARTLAND!
> THEN YOU CAN HAVE ALL
> THE WOMEN YOU WANT!

Martha scolds: "You better listen, dear, if you want to be a winner."

Mustard nods his head in agreement. He will take over Heartland, but the only woman he wants is the one sitting on that bale of hay in that barn. And he'll do *anything* to get her.

At the Heartland Weather Station, the Heartland barometer suddenly shifts from "fair" to "storms ahead." There is a visible chill in the air.

The Sgt. Pepper weathervane points nervously in the direction of the van. The rising wind makes it swing back and forth jerkily. The weathervane frowns. Trouble is brewing.

Sasha, Teacher Ellen's dog, dives under the couch. Ellen bends down and talks soothingly to her dog. The dog shakes uncontrollably.

Chickens scurry around their coops, making maddening circles. The cows moo like wolves and howl into the night. Something rotten is about to happen in the town of Heartland.

Mr. Kite sits in his office reading *The Annotated History of Sgt. Pepper*. His cigar suddenly tastes sour. Instinctively, he knows there is trouble out there. He may have arthritis, rheumatism and gout, but he'll fight to the end. He picks up a club and steps outside. He surveys the town from the Heartland City Hall steps. Something is definitely wrong. But where? He does not know.

A week goes by. At the other side of the United States, there's a part of Los Angeles called Century City. Century City is exactly the opposite of Heartland. The motto of Century City, after all, is: "Anything for the blessed buck!" Here, people are fabled for the amount of debt they can rack up. Many denizens think nothing of owing half a million dollars to their bank, credit association, psychiatrist, nutritionist, tennis instructor, tailor, automobile dealer and disco-dance instructor. After all, the only thing that matters in Century City is the making of the "deal." All day long the natives rush around discussing "deals, doing and undoing deal upon deal upon deal."

"How much will I make?" "How much is my advance?" "What's my percentage of the profits?" "How can I tax-shelter the money?" "Should I set up a trust fund?" These are the questions the natives of Century City ask over and over again.

When they are not dealing with deal-making, the natives are involved in the process of "evolving." They "become" by placing pyramids on their heads to gather the energies of the universe, attending est graduate sessions, plunging themselves into isolation tanks to hear their inner thoughts, attending holistic medical-training sessions, meditating with a wide variety of swamis and gurus, and getting their bodies "rolfed" to beat out the defensive postures of their youths, all of which replenish them so that they can go back to deal-making once again.

High atop two skyscraper towers in this city are the offices of the world's most powerful record company, Big Deal Records. A huge platinum long-playing record with a huge initial "B" embossed on it sits upon one of the towers; a huge platinum long-playing record with a huge initial "D" embossed on the label sits on top of the other. Between these letters is a huge, drooling sculpture of a snorting, red-faced, sacred pig. This is the Big Deal Records logo. A black cloud hangs perpetually over it.

Big Deal's fun-loving president, B.D. Brockhurst, makes his offices in the penthouse at the top of these towers. These offices are decorated predominantly in shades of platinum. The effect is one of tastelessness and flash—all pink fur cushions and fountains that spew forth sickeningly sweet pink champagne.

A strobe light flashes on a gigantic long-playing record with a picture of the snorting, red-faced, sacred pig in the center of it. It spins nonstop. This is B.D.'s desk. It never stops spinning because B.D. likes to think of himself as a man who's always on the move.

B.D. is dressed in a platinum-colored jumpsuit. Around his neck he wears dozens of platinum chains. In his ear is a platinum stickpin with a huge, bulbous diamond at the end of it. B.D. is not tasteful.

Look closely at his face and you may find that he does indeed resemble a snorting, red-faced, sacred pig. B.D. likes to drink champagne, chase after women, indulge in as much outrageous behavior as possible, while always appearing the good guy. He is as merry as he is monstrous.

B.D. had started out as a vacuum-cleaner salesman from Peoria. By swindling, cheating, bribing and sweet-talking, he now ruled an empire.

His first deputy assistant is the very sober Irvin Blomberg. Irvin has been nicknamed the "Evil Gladiola" by all of the employees at Big Deal Records. He has been given this nickname because he is not only a snake, but also because gladioli are always seen at funerals.

The Evil Gladiola does not look at all like his nickname. He wears crewneck sweaters, chino pants, and has a permanent Joe College smile. He maintains this expression by smearing gobs of makeup over himself each morning to disguise the damage done to his complexion by taking an inordinate amount of uppers and downers.

Permanently smiling, the Evil Gladiola is an especially skilled thief. His specialty is stealing the rights of all those who come into contact with Big Deal Records—especially those who are honest and talented.

Late at night, B.D. likes to sit with his smiling first deputy assistant. "How many innocent people have we screwed today?" B.D. usually asks merrily.

A wicked grin creeps over the Evil Gladiola's face. "Do you know that writer who really figured things out for us? We've stolen all his rights!

Once again, our teams of lawyers have done us proud!"

While thievery gave the Evil Gladiola great pleasure, the art of merchandising pleased him even more. At night, the Evil Gladiola would have dreams of bumper stickers, T-shirts, tacky costume jewelry, logos, jackets, posters, board games and comic books. There may be many people who view merchandisers with contempt, but the Evil Gladiola saw them as gods.

B.D. taps his fingers on the desk. He is famed for his magic fingers. When music makes his fingers tap, you can be sure that the music will become a number-one hit.

B.D. listens to the tape made by the Lonely Hearts Club Band. His fingers tap like crazy. He must sign this band to his recording label! He must sign them now! They have the sound of authentic superstars.

Across the room, also tapping her fingers, is B.D.'s leading recording artist, Lucy, who leads an especially trashy girls' group called Lucy and the Diamonds.

Lucy is so hot that steam pours onto B.D.'s contact lenses whenever he looks at her. With skin like spun silk, lips like melting cherries and eyes as piercing as those of a leopard in the night, Lucy is more woman than any man can handle.

When she was born, she had been so-o hot that the doctors had passed her back and forth in order not to burn their hands. Vapors of hot steam used to cloud her nursery window, and boy babies would struggle to crawl from their cribs toward her.

B.D. had met Lucy many years ago when he was selling vacuum cleaners and she was a teenager looking for her first set of wheels. He had found her oozing her way across the top of a T-Bird.

"Hi," she purred. "Your wheels just turn me on like crazy."

B.D. could hardly catch his breath. Her breasts heaved against the roof of the car.

"I think you better get down, young lady."

She slid down the car, which seemed to moan with rapture. Lucy then slid into B.D.'s arms. They had been together ever since.

Now he was B.D. Brockhurst, and she led a girls' group and did as B.D. said, and B.D. looked after her just fine.

Lucy's Diamonds are pretty hot, too. Nan Diamond busies herself trimming B.D.'s hair; Suki Diamond gives him a manicure; Debra Diamond shines his shoes. Each one could make any man's blood pressure shoot up twenty points.

Suddenly the Diamonds don't want to work on B.D. any longer. This music is driving them crazy. They jump up and begin boogying and "getting on down" to the magical sound.

Nan, Suki and Debra are movin' to the groove. "I can't stop dancing!" Nan exclaims. "And, Honey, I love it!"

B.D. loves it, too. Every track on this tape could be number one. Who are these boys? He takes out a picture of the band from an envelope, and he stares at it. Their look is perfect: innocent hicks. He hands the photo to Lucy.

Lucy carefully studies it. She focuses on Billy. She likes what she sees. So innocent-looking! So irresistible! Lucy licks her lips in anticipation. She can't wait to meet this child!

Debra grabs the picture from Lucy's hands. "Honey, I want that one!" She points to Mark. "He's got potential!"

Suki grabs the picture next. "Darling, wait a minute! That boy is mine!"

Nan casually takes the picture and slinks over to the platinum-colored couch. "I think I'll take them all!" she teases.

Suki and Debra leap up. "No you won't!" They're ready to fight!

B.D. presses a button and the drawer of a floor-to-ceiling, platinum-colored file flies open. It is filled with pictures of groups. They are filed under such categories as "Hopeless," "Cute, But Hopeless," "Able to Play at Least Three Chords," "Losers," "Nasty But Stands a Chance," "Dumb," "Dumber" and "Dumbest."

B.D. moves on to a file marked INSTANT SUPERSTARDOM. He takes the picture from the girls' hands and places it firmly in this file.

"This is going to be the biggest group in the history of popular music!" he announces as he slams the drawer shut.

Suddenly Lucy throws open the drawer once again. She removes the photograph. "You'll have to get another picture," she purrs. "This one belongs to me!" She runs her nails over Billy's face. B.D. smiles—he knows Lucy will be of great help to him.

B.D. reaches into the file and removes a mile-long contract. This is the contract devised by the Evil Gladiola in which Big Deal Records gets everything, and the artist gets nothing. It's the contract that B.D. is determined to get the Lonely Hearts Club Band to sign.

"I want him! I must have him!" Lucy moans, taking another peek at Billy.

"He's yours!" says Debra Diamond. "Meanwhile, we can't wait until we mess with the rest!"

B.D. laughs harshly. "And I can't wait until they're mine!"

Late that night, Charlie, the world's oldest Western Union Messenger, pedals up Heartland Hill to the Shears' barn. He clutches a telegram between his false teeth. As he nears the Shears' barn, familiar music is heard. It is the Lonely Hearts Club Band practicing, practicing, practicing! Dressed in nightclothes, the Heartlanders lean out of their windows to enjoy their late-evening serenade.

The bike's tire suddenly goes flat and Messenger Charlie tumbles to the ground. His teeth fall out of his mouth. The teeth, with the telegram tightly wedged between them, roll down Heartland Hill. Messenger Charlie follows bravely after them. He rescues his teeth, with the telegram still wedged between them.

Without a moment to lose, he runs with teeth and telegram in hand to the barn. He knows this has to be an important message. Who in Heartland ever got *two* telegrams in such a short time? Who in Heartland ever got two telegrams at all?

Messenger Charlie dashes into the barn. He can't talk, so he just hands his teeth to Dougie. Dougie holds them with disgust. He tries to retrieve the telegram from the teeth; the teeth, however, fight back. Mark helps by slowly wedging them open as Dougie carefully withdraws the telegram.

A restless Saralinda Shears looks out the window. She notices Messenger Charlie's bicycle. The telegram has arrived! She heads for the barn, with Ernest Shears following behind her.

The ducks in the pond stretch their short legs and eagerly shake their webbed feet. The cows nudge their calves. They all want to know what the telegram has to say.

Billy, Mark, Dave, Bob, Strawberry, Ernest and Saralinda, as well as the barnyard animals, gather around Dougie as he rips open the envelope. He reads out loud:

BIG DEAL LOVES YOUR TAPE. BIG DEAL LOVES YOU. EXPECT YOU IN L.A. TOMORROW.

SIGNED, B.D. BROCKHURST

Billy clasps Strawberry to him. The Henderson brothers hug each other. Saralinda throws her arms around Ernest. The ducks honk merrily; the chickens cackle happily.

And Bob uses Charlie's teeth as if they were castanets as Dave begins to dance with a cow.

And Dougie dreams of fame. . . . An enormous, lavish office! Eight telephones! Sixteen secretaries! Servants! Money—piles of it—everywhere! Dougie Shears: the world's most important rock 'n' roll manager.

"Manage me!" begs Elton John.

"Manage me!" begs Fleetwood Mac.

"Manage me!" begs Earth, Wind and Fire.

"Manage me!" begs Stevie Wonder.

The Heartland happiness swirls around Dougie, but all he can do is repeat to himself over and over again: "Billy is going to become a superstar, but I'm finally going to have power of my own!"

Billy and Strawberry are alone in the barn. They stand as one, afraid to move, afraid to leave one another's side. Gently, they kiss.

Finally, Billy breaks the silence. "I never loved you more than I love you now," he whispers. "Will you keep loving me? Without you I could never write another love song."

"I've never even thought about being without you," Strawberry muses. "You'll be a star. All the girls in Heartland are crazy about you already! Wait until the world catches a glimpse of you! Thousands of women . . ."

"It won't make any difference!"

A tear forms in Strawberry's eye. "You're not even gone and already I miss you."

Billy suddenly grabs her hand. "Come on!"

"Where are we going?"

"We're going to have one fabulous last night together—a night to keep in our memories that will last us and always keep us together!"

To cheer her up, Billy begins to sing a tune of his that always reminds him of the love he and Strawberry so deeply feel for each other.

The long and winding road that
   leads to your door
Will never disappear, I've seen
   that road before
It always leads me here
Leads me to your door

Many times I've been alone
Many times I've cried

Anyway you'll never know the
   many ways I've tried

But still they lead me back to
   the long, winding road
You left me standing here, a
   long, long time ago
Don't leave me waiting here
Lead me to your door.

The wild and windy night
That the rain washed away
Has left a pool of tears crying
   for the day
Why leave me standing here
Let me know the way

Many times I've been alone,
   many times I've cried
Anyway you'll never know the
   many ways I've tried

But still they lead me back to
   the long winding road
You left me standing here a
   long, long time ago
Don't leave me waiting here
Lead me to your door.

Mr. Mustard scowls. He has been monitoring
Billy and Strawberry on his periscope. It is indeed
wonderful that this wretched rock 'n' roller is
leaving for Los Angeles. Then Strawberry will
definitely be his!

But now Strawberry and Billy are headed into

the night. They're holding hands. They love each other! Nightmare of nightmares!

Barbra beeps angrily at Mr. Mustard, "Mustard, baby, keep your mind on business!"

Martha beeps snappily, "Sweetness, you're here to ruin Heartland, not to fool around with local chickadees!"

But Mr. Mustard can't get his mind off this ravishing maiden.

"Mustard," belches Irma, "pay attention to us!"

Mr. Mustard scowls. He turns and bumps his head on the periscope. "Shut up!" he screams. "You are three of the noisiest computers I've ever dealt with! Shut up, or I'll rip out your tubes!"

Only the sight of Strawberry calms him down. He punches the close-up button; Strawberry comes into focus. Soon, he is drooling happily again.

Billy and Strawberry run through the fields. "I love you, Strawberry Fields!" Billy shouts as they frolic together.

"And I love you, Billy Shears!"

"Are you with me?" Billy yells as he starts to run into the water.

Strawberry follows him into the pond. "All the way!"

They stand in the pond amidst the honking ducks.

Billy takes Strawberry in his arms and holds her close and tight.

He looks down at her face. Tears form in her eyes.

She smiles sweetly. "I'm with you, Billy!"

Billy nods. "All the way!"

They kiss and hold each other so hard that they fall backward into the pond. They rock with laughter. Both swim to the edge and crawl up on the dry grass. Suddenly Strawberry jumps up and starts running.

"Where are you going?"

"Are you with me?" she calls.

Billy runs after her. "All the way!" He tries to grab her, but she dodges him. He starts to run the other way.

She calls after him. "Hey you, come back here!"

Billy scoots back. "Yes?"

"I miss you already!" She buries her head in his shoulder.

He holds her tight. They are both shivering. Billy takes Strawberry's hand. "I think we'd better get into some dry clothes."

"I want some chocolate ice-cream."

"You've got it!"

They run back toward the farm. Mustard does not miss a moment of it. They get farther and farther away. Mustard turns and glowers at a grinning Irma. He marches over to the computerette and gives her a well-placed kick in a left transistor.

"Brute!" he shouts. "Closer!" The van lunges forward and speeds toward the barn.

Mr. Mustard screams, "Stop!" The van stops immediately. Mr. Mustard and the computerettes fly across the van and knock against each other. They all land on the ground.

Barbra picks herself up. "Mustard, baby, I think maybe you could use another driver!"

Mr. Mustard runs to the front of the van. He starts to push the boxing-glove button, but then he decides to try another approach to make his idiot driver respond. "Brute, I want you to slowly, carefully, and quietly follow that young couple. Is that too hard to understand?"

"No siree bob." Brute starts the van up again, but with much more care than usual this time.

Mr. Mustard is pleased with himself. Sometimes, against all odds, kindness does work.

Billy and Strawberry sit in the barn gobbling chocolate ice-cream and chocolate-chip cookies. They are both getting sleepy.

"Aren't they disgusting?" Mustard says to himself as he watches their every move on the videoscreen.

Brute suddenly puts his foot on the gas pedal. The van heads for the barn door!

"Stop! Stop!" screams Mustard.

The van comes to a screeching halt. Two inches more and it would have been in Strawberry's lap!

Mr. Mustard runs to the front of the van and pushes the punch button. Brute is smacked square in the face. Mr. Mustard pushes the button again. Once again, Brute is punched. Again . . . and again . . . and again! Mustard loves pushing the button; Brute loves getting hit. What a happy couple they make!

Billy and Strawberry are perched on a hay block. Billy puts a chocolate-chip cookie in his mouth. Strawberry takes it from him. "Let me do that." She holds the cookie as he takes a bite. They each take spoons and feed each other ice-cream.

Billy misses her mouth and they laugh. "This reminds me of when you were a little girl and you had the measles. Remember?"

"Sure. I even wrote it down in my diary. December 2: Dear Diary, Today I am very sick with the measles. But Billy visited me and fed me soup. He kissed me for the very first time. Dear Diary, I think I love him.' "

Billy reaches into his pocket, takes out a small box, opens it, and hands a silver coin to Strawberry. "This is more than just a silver dollar. It's the coin Grandfather Pepper put in my hand on the day I was born. I was going to hand it down to my first son. You take it and someday you will be the one to hand it to our son."

Strawberry throws her arms around Billy's neck.

"Strawberry, even though I'm leaving, you know that I want us to be together—always, forever." Billy looks away. Now he does not want to go to L.A.

"Let's not talk any more about your going." She knows how tortured Billy is at the moment. She doesn't want to make it harder.

Billy is relieved to change the subject. "Okay, let's talk about the children we're going to have."

Strawberry sits cross-legged, like an eager child. "How many do you want?"

"Two and a half."

"Two and a half?"

"That's how many children the average couple has in America these days."

"We're better than average," Strawberry says defensively. "We're from Heartland, you know."

"Make it five!"

"Five? That's too many!"

"Well, Strawberry Fields Shears, how many do you suggest?"

"Strawberry Fields Shears," Strawberry whispers. "That sounds terrific." She nestles in his arms as Billy gently rocks her. They have never been closer. They talk some more and then grow quiet as they imagine the happy future they will share together.

Suddenly Strawberry is asleep. And soon Billy is too.

They dream of each other and the extraordinary love they share between them. Neither wants the morning to come, even though they know it will. Neither wants the dream to end!

FOUR

A symphony of roosters vigorously begins to crow. Ducks flap their wings in the pond. A brilliant red sun rises in the East.

Morning over Heartland!

The day begins in a burst of song:

> Here comes the sun
> Here comes the sun
> And I say—It's all right
> Little Darling, it's been a long,
>   cold, lonely winter
> Little Darling, it feels like
>   years since it's been here,
> Here comes the sun
> Here comes the sun
> And I say—it's all right.
>
> Little Darling, the smiles
>   returning to the faces
> Little Darling, it seems like
>   years since it's been here

Here comes the sun
Here comes the sun
And I say—it's all right.

Sun, sun, sun, here it comes
Sun, sun, sun, here it comes
Sun, sun, sun, here it comes
Sun, sun, sun, here it comes.

Here comes the sun
Here comes the sun
It's all right, it's all right.

A family of chirping, hungry robins settles on the van. They chirp so loudly that they awaken Mr. Mustard, who has fallen asleep at his periscope. He looks up and sees a mother robin feeding her baby a worm.

"Ugh!" he growls. His back is stiff; he aches all over. He turns to the videoscreen and stares at it through red-rimmed eyes. "They're still in the barn!" he exclaims. "Damn!" He drops the periscope on his foot.

Strawberry is cuddled in Billy's arms. She nuzzles her nose in his neck. Half asleep, she whispers, "I love the way you feel, Billy Shears!"

The calves feed from their mothers. Chicks chirp for their morning meal. A morning dove coos happily. Its sound makes Billy stir. And then Strawberry realizes that Billy is about to leave her. "Every morning from now on, whenever I hear the morning dove, I'll think of your leaving," she says quietly.

They melt into a warm, lingering good-morning kiss. Suddenly, Billy realizes that it's time to go. He jumps up and grabs Strawberry's arm. She tries to be brave, but it's hard. "I just never really believed it until now. I still don't believe it." Strawberry holds back tears. Sobs rise from her throat, but she fights them back.

"Hold me long and tight!" says Billy. "One last time!"

They both hold each other so tight that they ache. Strawberry smiles bravely. Then Billy takes her hand and they dash from the barn and jump into the pick-up truck. They drive past Mr. Mustard's van.

"Good-bye, Billy Shears!" Mr. Mustard says gleefully as the truck roars off. "And good morning, Strawberry Mustard!"

In the town square, Mark, Dave, Bob, Dougie, Saralinda and Ernest Shears, the Hendersons and a few other townspeople wait nervously for Billy. The silly girls and brashy boys are also there. The rest of Heartland watches from windows and doorways. Mr. Kite stands proudly on the steps of Heartland City Hall. He looks up at the Sgt. Pepper weathervane and winks. The weathervane winks back.

Years ago when Sgt. Pepper had gone off to fight in the first Great War, he had departed in the Heartland Hot-Air Balloon. At that time a hot-air balloon had been the most newfangled way to travel. Now, to celebrate that historic journey, the Heartland Hot-Air Balloon has once again been unfurled—this time for Sgt. Pepper's grandson.

Bob Henderson stares at the balloon. He has never traveled in a balloon before, and after the balloon ride he'll have to travel in a jet. He's already air sick, even though he's still on the ground.

Dougie does a last-minute check on the airline tickets, travelers' checks and luggage. Soon he will be in L.A. Soon he will have the power he craves.

Suddenly Mimi squeals, "Here comes Billy!"

The truck pulls up. Billy jumps out. He turns to give Strawberry a helping hand. They give each other yet another final hug.

Dougie scowls. "Hurry up, Billy! You've already made us late!"

"Are you with me?" Billy asks Strawberry.

"All the way!"

Billy hugs his weeping mother. He hugs his strangely silent dad. He shakes the hand of Mr. Kite, who slaps him on the back. He looks up at the Sgt. Pepper weathervane, and the weathervane gives him courage. Then he climbs into the balloon.

Before anyone can say anything, the balloon takes off into the sky. The Heartlanders weep for joy at the sight of this extraordinary moment.

"So long, Billy," calls Ernest as he breaks his silence. "I love you very much!"

Zena Henderson makes one final plea to her sons. "Get a lot of sleep and plenty to eat. And don't take any funny pills!"

"You boys bring me back some new stories to tell!" shouts a grinning Mr. Kite.

The silly girls jump up and down. "We love Sgt. Pepper's Lonely Hearts Club Band! We love Sgt. Pepper's Lonely Hearts Club Band!" they cheer.

The balloon climbs higher and higher. The sky has never been bluer as it embraces the gaily painted balloon.

Billy peers over its side. Strawberry is now a little speck on the ground. He feels a twinge in his heart. He already misses her.

On the ground, everyone stares up into the sky.

Merrily, the Heartlanders congratulate each other. Today five of their best representatives have been sent into the world. It makes them proud.

Only Strawberry is left alone. She watches the little balloon being swallowed up into the white clouds. She can hold back her tears no longer. She sobs and sobs and sobs.

At Centerville Municipal Airport, the boys dock their balloon and climb aboard a superjet.

B.D. has sent them first-class tickets and informed the airline that they are to be treated like kings.

Adoring stewardesses outfitted in tight nylon T-shirts and tight, clinging, above-the-knee skirts immediately surround them.

A wet-lipped stewardess waits on Mark. "Honey, would you like a drink or something?" She presses against Mark's thigh.

Mark breaks out in a fit of blushes. "No thank you, ma'am," he replies.

Bob, however, is not nearly so shy. "What have you got for me?" he asks.

The stewardess throws him a dirty look. "How about a double Shirley Temple, sonny?"

Bob grins. "Anything you've got I'll take!"

She turns on her heel and marches off.

Bob appreciatively watches her wiggle.

Meanwhile, Dave shows his card tricks to the two nuns sitting next to him. And Mark fights off an endless procession of girls while Bob hangs in there for the leftovers.

The atmosphere certainly is different from Heartland. A soft-core musical is shown on the plane's movie screen. Mark, Dave and Bob look around nervously every once in a while to see if anyone is watching them watch it. Then they turn back to the screen.

Billy, however, only stares into space, remembering the fragrance of Strawberry.

And Dougie is busy getting tips on the stock market from an oil tycoon he's met at the bar.

The entire staff of B.D. Records is gathered in front of B.D. B.D. clicks off a number of orders one by one.

"Franny, I want every restaurant to know the boys by sight. They are to be treated like royalty whenever they go out. . . . Harris, open charge accounts for them in all the best stores in Beverly Hills. Encourage them to spend. The more they spend, the more they'll be in debt to me. . . . Sammy, I want the most elaborate instruments and equipment money can buy. . . . Franny, be sure that the music trade papers cover every move they make. I want them impressed by the amount of press coverage they receive. . . . Vivian, stock their hotel room with booze and drugs. The more stoned they are, the more I'll get my way. . . . Now, all of you, get to it!"

The room empties except for Lucy, the Diamonds and the Evil Gladiola. B.D. addresses Lucy and the Diamonds. "And you know your job!" he snaps.

The four women nod their heads affirmatively. They not only know their job, but they also know how good they are at it. And they can't wait to ply their trade on these Heartland hicks—each and every one a bona fide cutie.

The Evil Gladiola paces back and forth with his calculator in hand. "I have a list of women whom the boys should be seen with—Diana Ross, Bette

Midler, Farah Fawcett-Majors. . . . Is she still married?"

B.D. nods affirmatively

"Okay, there are plenty more—Olivia Newton-John, Rita Coolidge, Barbra Streisand . . . no, she's busy. . . . Tatum O'Neal . . ."

B.D. interrupts: "Too young. . . ."

And on into the night, the merry pair plots and plots and plots. Never have any two so much enjoyed being so rotten!

FIVE

The jet touches down at Los Angeles International Airport at four that afternoon. Billy, Mark, Dave, Bob and Dougie step off the plane. Their eyes pop open as they survey the hubbub.

Suddenly a huge platinum-colored limousine drives across the airstrip. It heads directly for them. The car tires are huge, shining, spinning L.P.'s. On the car's hood is painted the huge, snorting, red-faced, sacred pig.

The boys stare at the car. They are astonished by it, as well as by its driver, Lucy. She is dressed in a glittering, platinum chauffeur's costume. The sun makes her shimmer. She stares at the boys and she begins to purr and growl. Then she smacks the ground with her whip. The boys jump.

Billy graciously extends his hand and says, "I'm Billy Shears. How do you do?"

Lucy lunges toward him and presses her body against his. "I'm Lucy, and everything I do, I do very well!"

B.D. clears his throat to get their attention.

Lucy flings open the car door. B.D. steps out.

"I'm B.D.," chortles the world's most powerful record company president. He extends his hand.

Dougie sees dollar signs rolling in B.D.'s eyes. He hears the clanging of cash-register bells as they clasp hands. From the feel of Dougie's fingers, B.D. immediately knows that this boy will do everything he asks of him.

B.D. shakes hands with the rest of the group and delivers a warm smile. Sunlight glints off his gold tooth. The air is scented with the smell of bay rum.

Instinctively, Billy smells a skunk. He looks up. Lucy is staring hungrily at him in the rearview mirror. Billy turns away.

Meanwhile Bob is enthralled by the limousine. He scurries under it to check it out. "There's no grease. How can a car be so clean?" he asks with genuine curiosity.

B.D. shudders. Superstars don't climb under cars. "Lucy, my dear, please ask our guest to get *in* the car and *not* under it."

Lucy doesn't respond. She can't take her eyes off the reflection of Billy. She is already thinking about her next move.

B.D. growls, "At once!"

Lucy climbs out of the car and gets down on her hands and knees. "Bob, baby," she purrs, "come out. I've got things to show you that are much more exciting than some dirty old car parts." She shimmies suggestively.

Bob looks up at Lucy and bumps his head on the car. She winks at him; she is hypnotic. He chokes. "Oh, well, I can look under a car any old time."

With everyone back in the car, B.D. instantly unfurls the huge contract. He takes a platinum-colored fountain pen from his jacket. There is a coaxing grin on his face. "All right, boys, who wants to be the first to sign up with me?"

A song runs through B.D.'s mind as he begins to cajole the boys:

I want you
I want you so bad
I want you
I want you so bad it's driving
    me mad
It's driving me mad.

I want you
I want you so bad, babe
I want you
I want you so bad it's driving
    me mad
It's driving me mad.

I want you
I want you so bad
I want you so bad it's driving
    me mad
It's driving me mad.

She's so heavy [heavy] heavy
[She's so] heavy, heavy . . .

I want you
I want you so bad
I want you so bad it's driving
    me mad
It's driving me mad.

I want you
I want you so bad, babe
I want you so bad it's driving
    me mad
It's driving me mad
You know I want you so bad
I want you so bad it's driving
    me mad.

I want you
I want you so bad
It's driving me mad, it's
    driving me mad.

B.D. squeezes Dougie's hand appreciatively. He next hands the contract to Billy. Billy looks at it. He looks at B.D. He is skeptical. "No, I'm not ready for a contract," he says firmly.

The other boys stick with Billy's decision. Billy's instincts have always been right.

The limousine pulls away, headed for the freeway. Dougie catches Lucy's eye in the rearview mirror. She gapes lustfully at Billy. Dougie tries to catch her eye. Lucy throws Dougie a who-are-you-kidding look, then turns back to Billy. She has trouble keeping her hands off him.

Not this woman too, thinks Dougie. Billy has Strawberry. This woman is the most thrilling woman he's ever seen. Why does he want her too? She's got to be mine.

B.D.'s limousine is equipped with individual television sets, tape decks, telephones and bars for each of the boys. The boys eagerly play with all of the toys.

They gaze out the window at their new home—this place called Los Angeles.

The boys stare out the front window, side windows and rear window of the limousine. They can't believe their eyes. Cars everywhere. Bumper to bumper down the San Diego Freeway toward Hollywood. The speed limit reads 55 miles per hour, but the traffic moves at half that rate. And garbage, bottles and paper are strewn everywhere. The street lights are switched on because the smog is so thick and the black cloud overhead refuses to disappear.

Bob shakes his head in disbelief. "I think I understand why Mom was worried."

B.D. laughs. "Nothing to worry about, boys; you'll be well taken care of!"

The exhaust fumes from the car are stifling, and B.D. turns on the air conditioner to quell everyone's tearing eyes.

A car suddenly stalls in the left lane, but the other cars don't stop moving; they just push against it until it is whisked along by sheer momentum.

The boys duck under the seat at the sight—all except Dougie, who is glowing with delight.

Lucy leaves the freeway and turns onto Sunset Boulevard. For the first time, the boys catch a glimpse of the fabled "Sunset Strip."

B.D. opens his arms. "Well, boys, this is it— the home of all the greatest rock stars—the street of the Roxy, the Whiskey, Tower Records!"

But now hundreds of young, heavily made-up women line each side of the street. And all of them are hitchhiking.

"I wonder why so many young girls don't have their own cars," Billy says out loud.

The limo continues slowly down the street, trying to avoid the religious fanatics running from vehicle to vehicle.

"Save your soul by praying to Big Ed!" screams one.

"Sinners, kill yourself now! That's the Christian way to solve overpopulation!"

The limo comes to an eight-way intersection caught in the midst of an incredible traffic snarl. The boys are deafened by the sound of car horns.

By this time, the smog is so thick that Lucy has to turn on the window wipers just to remove the filth from the windshield.

The boys look up through the smog at the huge billboards that dominate the landscape. They see a naked Geisha girl carrying a suitcase on which a huge pasted sticker reads:

COME FEEL THE ORIENT WITH ME!

Another billboard features five of the meanest-looking kids the Lonely Hearts Club Band have ever seen. They have green hair and wear rings through their noses. The picture is captioned:

SUCKER—NOW LIVE AT THE FORUM

Another billboard shows a lovely young couple lighting each other's cigarettes:

I SMOKE A CIGARETTE FOR THE
SUCCESSFUL FEELING IT BRINGS ME.
FEEL GOOD WITH "WEEDS."

Dougie loves it all. "This sure isn't Heartland!" he exclaims.

A disappointed Billy replies, "It isn't!"

On every corner there's a fast-food stand—"Duck Donald's," "Jump-in-the-Box," "Hamburger Hustle," "Todd's Little Girl," "Der Wiener," "The Thousand and One Flavors" and one called "Tacky-Taco."

Vendors approach the car, hustling their fast food in the streets.

Dave grabs a Tacky-Taco. But the stench makes everyone choke. B.D. dumps it out the window. It burns a hole in the pavement.

"Save your stomach, son. You'll be eating very shortly. And you'll be eating in the style to which you'll soon be accustomed!"

No one eats anything like this in Heartland, thinks Billy. These people must all have nutritional diseases—beriberi, scurvy, even the dreaded rickets!

Everywhere kids hustle maps to the homes of the rock heavies.

Suddenly, in a roar of exhaust fumes, a motorcycle escort surrounds the limousine. On each motorcycle is one of Lucy's Diamonds done up like sexy Hell's Angels—all leather, chains and skull-and-crossbone tattoos.

"Boys, these are my women!" Lucy says proudly.

The boys peer at the Diamonds, who blow kisses to them as they swing their chains over their heads like suggestive lassos.

Once again, B.D. hands the contract to Billy. Billy smiles politely and once again shakes his head no! Billy then notices that Lucy is still staring at him. She mouths the word "Yummy."

Embarrassed, he turns to look out the window of the car, but the Diamonds have pressed their breasts up against it and he can see nothing but heaving, steamy breasts.

The limousine now turns down Santa Monica Boulevard. The small buildings are all painted red and black. Beady-eyed men lurk in corners or thumb through paperbacks and magazines at the dirty bookstores. Tall barkers entice young boys into peep shows. "Everything you've always wanted to see and more! Don't listen to rumors, boys! Once you've seen one, you haven't seen all! Come on in!"

Curvacious women pull old men by their belt buckles into massage parlors. In the window of one of the parlors loiter three scantily clad masseuses. Somehow they look just like the Diamonds!

The girls crook their fingers and wink at the boys.

The boys open the car window to get a better look. The smog makes them gag; tears roll from their eyes.

Finally the limousine pulls into chic Beverly Hills. The limousine is suddenly engulfed in a sea of Rolls-Royces, Mercedes Benzes, Bentleys, Jaguars, Stutzes, Panteras, Cords, Sevilles and Jensens—all painted black, of course, not to show the dirt.

Each shop in this district is more extravagant than the last. There are poodle salons, gourmet spice stores, silk-spun-while-you-wait shops, wash-your-money launderettes.

People stroll down the sidewalk pushing shopping carts filled with money. Matrons pass each other in the street and admire the size of each other's credit-card necklaces.

A policeman knocks on the window of the car and hands each of the boys a brochure. It explains the pricing system in Beverly Hills. It reads:

Don't drive on Beverly unless you can afford to spend at least one hundred dollars per item; on Rexford, nothing costs less than five hundred dollars—stay off it if you don't have the bread; on Rodeo Drive, one thousand dollars is the minimum cost per item; and if that makes you nervous, then pack up your bags and go home!

Turning up Rodeo, the limo stops at a red light in front of the Super Show-Off Jewelry Shop. Billy is dazzled by the glittering array of huge, chunky, blue-white diamonds in the window.

Suddenly the mannequins holding these jewels come to life. Billy blinks; *they are the Diamonds!* They entice the boys with gold bracelets, star sapphires and glittering ruby necklaces.

Suddenly, the Diamonds are in every store window on the Drive. They offer the boys tailored white linen suits, hand-stitched Italian boots, form-fitting French jeans and elegant, flowing silk scarves. "All of Gucci will be yours!" they cheer.

Dave tries to open the car door, but Lucy's got them locked in.

B.D. laughs hard and loud. He puffs on a chartreuse-colored Sherman cigarillo. He hands Dave the contract. Dave immediately signs it. Why not? He doesn't know what a "Gucci" is, but that doesn't mean he won't like it when he gets it.

The limo eventually pulls up to B.D.'s mansion. B.D. serves as tour guide as the car rolls around the grounds. The boys stare bug-eyed at the imported trees and shrubs, streams, fountains, Oriental bridges, bonsai forests, mile-high redwood groves, waterfalls, mini-rapids, suspension bridges, vast pools stocked with two-foot-long goldfish, golf and tennis courts, ice-skating pond, monkey house, horse stable, and small jungle replete with peacocks, performing monkeys and hula girls serving mai-tais. This is what B.D. calls home.

Lucy takes Billy's arm. "I'd like to make you comfortable," she coos. Billy sinks into Lucy's arms, overwhelmed by this paradise into which he has stumbled.

The Diamonds drape themselves over Mark, Dave and Bob.

Servants appear carrying giant magnums of champagne and fifty-pound tins of caviar.

The boys swim, sun, drink and enjoy the sauna and hot tubs, tennis, horseback riding, hockey and skeet-shooting. They even engage in a round of camp songs. Beautiful people drift in and out, existing only to create atmosphere. Dozens of beauties clad in the tiniest of bikinis lounge all over the grounds. And Lucy and her Diamonds never leave the boys for a minute, anticipating and then fulfilling all of their wishes.

As the sun sets, B.D. claps his hands. An enormous backdrop of Heartland, featuring Heartland City Hall, appears from seemingly nowhere. The boys step into this floor-to-ceiling tableau. This is their "signing" picture, heralding the fact that they have signed a contract making them part of the label forever. It will appear on the cover of all of the music trade papers as soon as B.D. can get them all to sign that contract.

Lucy stands with her Nikon shooting the photographs while B.D. does some very fast talking. "This is the advertising campaign, boys," he says speedily. "Four boys from Heartland, U.S.A.—innocent, young and extremely talented. Suddenly you meet me—world-famous, all-powerful me. And I convert you into the biggest stars in rock history! You'll be famous everywhere. Women will grovel at your feet! You'll live a life of luxury beyond your wildest expectations! Even beyond all this!"

B.D. again claps his hands. Lucy and her Diamonds appear with lavish red sequined costumes. Servants appear with fur coats, fur hats and fur pants. Lucy drives up in a platinum Jaguar! Televisions, stereos, and skis are tossed onto the lawn. Suddenly a small yacht appears on B.D.'s lake. Moving men appear and unload the world's most expensive guitars, amplifiers, speakers, microphones, synthesizers and other hot-shot music equipment.

B.D. beams. "Boys, all this can be yours. And the price is right! Just sign on the dotted line."

Servants continue to bring out more costumes: rhinestone ones, velvet ones, gold, satin ones, tuxedos, jean suits. More. More. More. The boys change into and out of them while Lucy merrily snaps pictures of them.

B.D. once again claps his hands. The Heartland backdrop flies up. Behind it is an elegant candlelit banquet. Servant after servant appears with trays of the most elegantly prepared dishes and bottles of the world's rarest wines.

During dinner, B.D. takes a huge bankroll out of his pocket. He stuffs Dougie's pockets with money. Dougie grins angelically. This is heaven and B.D. is Santa Claus!

Debra Diamond chews on Mark's ears as the servants drape him with gold and silver chains. Nan Diamond slips mink slippers onto his feet as she kisses each toe. Suki Diamond dances seductively in front of him, taunting and begging him to dance with her. B.D. drops hundreds of dollar bills over his head and waves the contract in front of Mark's face. This is no time to be rational. Mark grabs the contract and signs it eagerly.

As a waiter pours Billy yet another glass of champagne, B.D. makes another stab. He offers Billy the contract. Once again, Billy pushes it away. His head aches, he is dizzy and numb, but he still knows right from wrong, and he does not trust B.D.

Once again B.D. claps his hands. The living room of his mansion is now a throbbing disco. Music crashes down upon the boys as they are assaulted by a battery of flashing lights.

The room is garnished by Los Angeles' beautiful people, dressed in outrageous costumes.

Lounging at the bar are Elton John, Farrah Fawcett-Majors, John Travolta, Barbra Streisand, Sylvester Stallone, Liza Minnelli, Ringo, Michelle Phillips, Joni Mitchell and two of the Eagles. They all wave and throw kisses at B.D., and B.D. gleefully throws kisses back.

Everybody dances wildly, thrusting their bodies into an endless series of exotic postures.

Mark, Dave and Bob cavort wildly on the dance floor with the Diamonds.

When Billy is not looking, B.D. drops a giant white pill into Billy's drink. The pill has a number embossed on it.

Billy sips his drink and instantly feels woozy. He staggers around the room. The room moves faster than he does.

B.D. nods to Lucy. "Come with me, sugar." She leads Billy out the door.

"Is everything all right?" he murmurs.

"You're doing everything just fine! Just follow Mama," Lucy whispers. "Mama's gonna make everything even better."

"Is my mama here?"

Lucy leads Billy to B.D.'s private chambers. As she guides him through the room, she casually starts kissing the tips of his fingers. In the center of the room is a huge circular couch in the shape of a long-playing Big Deal record. Lucy leads him to the couch. Billy lands straight on the snorting, red-faced, sacred pig logo.

Lucy removes his shoes and socks; she nibbles on his toes. She removes his jacket and bites his shoulders. She blows violently in his ears.

Suddenly the couch begins to spin and Lucy is on top of Billy. She covers him with bites and scratches.

A mile-long document swirls up around him like a set of chains coming to life. It is the contract. Billy can't focus on a thing. Lucy puts a platinum pen into his hand. She guides Billy's hand. Slowly, he scratches the name "B-i-l-l-y S-h-e-a-r-s" on the dotted line. A triumphant Lucy presses her mouth against his.

Billy twists and turns. He wants to move, but he is too paralyzed; he is too drugged. A hiss of steam covers his face.

He lets out a piercing scream. Agony? Ecstasy? Now he is too far gone to know the difference!

SIX

Dawn. The next day. A busy Dougie roams Sunset Boulevard pasting up posters. They read:

THE LONELY HEARTS CLUB BAND!
THEIR FIRST ALBUM DUE ANY DAY!

The streets are bursting with energy. The rhythm of the traffic is so intense that Dougie immediately begins to compose a tune in his head. He thinks that maybe he too is destined to be a superstar. As he walks down Sunset Boulevard, he sings out loud:

> Nothing to do to save his life
> Call his wife in
> Nothing to say but what a day
> How's your boy been
> Nothing to do. It's up to you
> I've got nothing to say but it's
>   okay

Good morning, good morning,
good morning.

Good morning, good morning,
good morning.

Going to work don't want to go
feeling low down
Heading for home you start to roam
Then you're in town
Everybody knows there's nothing
doing
Everything is closed, it's like
a ruin
Everyone you see is half asleep
And you're on your own
You're in the street
After a while you start to smile
Now you feel cool
Then you decide to take a walk
by the old school
Nothing has changed, it's still
the same
I've got nothing to say but it's
okay.

Good morning, good morning,
good morning.

People running around it's five
o'clock
Everywhere in town it's getting
dark
Everyone you see is full of life
It's time for tea and meet the
wife.

Somebody needs to know the time
Glad that I'm here
Watching the skirts you start
   to flirt
Now you're in gear.

Go to a show you hope she goes
I've got nothing to say but it's
   okay
Good morning, good morning,
   good morning.

Good morning, good morning,
   good morning!

Dougie runs from car to car. To each driver he announces, "The Lonely Hearts Club Band! Remember that name! They're the newest and most sensational rock group ever!"

With B.D.'s support, Dougie knows that the Lonely Hearts Club Band is going to reach superstar status. And he is their manager! He will be a superstar too!

He stares at the posters and blinks. Suddenly he visualizes them reading:

DOUGIE SHEARS PRESENTS
SGT. PEPPER'S
LONELY HEARTS CLUB BAND!

Yes, he will have equal billing, and if he plays his cards right, he will also have all the money! After all, what these boys don't know won't hurt them. And they don't know how rotten he really is!

And then Lucy will come crawling to *him*. But would he have her? After all, with all that fame

Sgt. Pepper's Lonely Hearts Club Band had a certain magic about them; it's why soldiers laid down their arms the minute they heard their merry sound.

Mr. Kite had been Mayor of Heartland for 43 years. He had run on the progressive ticket promising more sunshine, happiness and merriment. He also had been appointed guardian of Sgt. Pepper's musical instruments.

It was a fair day in Heartland and the highlight of the fair was Sgt. Pepper's Lonely Hearts Club Band. What a day for fun, music, magic and the letting go of balloons!

Superstardom beckons! The boys receive a telegram from Big Deal Records, the world's most powerful record company. "Send us a tape immediately," urges the record label.

Billy's stepbrother, Dougie Shears, had an infectious smile but a terrible case of greed. He'd do anything to get what Billy had—and he did!

Mean Mr. Mustard was a loser. Now he was going to be a winner. He would not only take over Heartland, but also get the girl—Billy's!

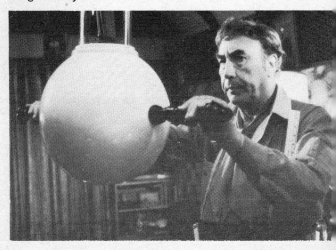

The Heartland hot-air balloon had been the means Sgt. Pepper had used to travel to Europe during World War I. Now it would take his grandson Billy to Los Angeles and the "Big Time."

The boys arrive in Los Angeles not knowing of the corruption that awaits them.

B. D. Brockhurst had to make the Lonely Hearts Club Band sign his contract. It would give him everything and them nothing.

Mustard and the Brute steal the instruments. Heartland immediately goes punk.

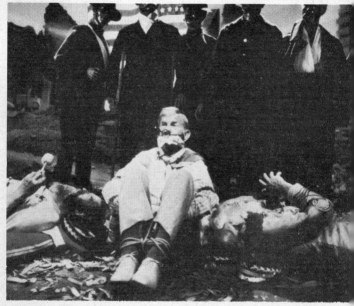

The instruments are gone. Will Heartland be saved and by whom? A black cloud forms over this ideal town.

Strawberry flees to Los Angeles to tell Billy of the tragedy that has struck their beloved homeland.

Late at night, while Los Angeles sleeps, the billboards high above Sunset Strip come to life, especially if they feature the musical act acclaimed by everybody as pure trash—Lucy and her Diamonds.

Sgt. Pepper's Lonely Hearts Club Band cuts its first platinum single. Experts agree that no new band has ever learned recording techniques so quickly.

Mr. Maxwell Edison—a loser if ever there was one—now has the power to turn old losers into young ones—courtesy of Sgt. Pepper's magical instruments.

Father Sun preaches the joys of greed at the infamous Temple of Cosmology on Hollywood Boulevard.

The Lonely Hearts Club Band comes home, and even Mr. Kite gets into the act.

Dougie Shears and Lucy join forces to steal the benefits of the Benefit. Thieving turns them on!

Earth, Wind & Fire, always ready to give its all to any worthy cause, come to Heartland to perform at the Benefit for Mr. Kite.

The Future Villain Band, consumed by pure hatred, uses Sgt. Pepper's instruments to raise an army to take over the world.

Heartland's heart breaks after Strawberry Fields sacrifices herself for the boy she loves.

Sgt. Pepper comes to life to make sure that good triumphs over evil and that everyone lives happily ever after.

Strawberry is brought back to life to rejoin her beloved Billy.

"Let us all be the stars of our dreams," declares Sgt. Pepper, and as our fable ends all of Heartland has been converted into the world's most famous band.

and riches, he will be able to have anybody. And everybody!

B.D.'s limousine, driven by Lucy, pulls up to the entrance of the Continental Hyatt House, the hotel where all new bands stay when they come to L.A.

The boys, red-eyed, exhausted, wasted and hung over, climb into the car. Lucy sits next to Billy. She presses against his thigh. He is too tired to feel a thing.

They zoom out into Sunset Boulevard past the Hyatt House marquee, which reads:

WELCOME, LONELY HEARTS
CLUB BAND!

The sign serves as a shot of energy. The boys are amazed to see their names so prominently displayed.

The car pulls up to Tower Records—one of the world's best-known record stores. Dougie has just plastered the front of it with posters. The boys are very much impressed.

"Onward to the recording studio to cut our first hit album," Dougie commandeers. He jumps into the limo and the car zooms off.

In the studio, the boys are given coffee and then introduced to their engineer, Easy Mix Jack. They are amazed by the huge, complicated recording board, a maze of dials and flashing lights. Inside the studio they are shown how the sound they make can be given doses of "echo," "reverberation," and "phasing," making it sound just like the whoosh of a jet plane.

Then their voices are "doubled" and "tripled,"

making them sound like eight, then twelve, men. They are also taught how to "solo a track," so that each can do his part separately, the parts then being blended into a perfect whole.

The boys can hardly believe their own ears. They can sound a million different ways.

They can't wait to attempt the professional recording process. They eagerly wait for instructions.

"Okay, boys. Take one," announces Easy Mix Jack.

Billy calls out, "One-two, one-two-three . . ."

The band starts up. Suddenly Dave's voice cracks from nervousness.

Easy Mix Jack talks to them over the microphone. "Relax. It's painless. Catch your breath and let's begin again."

Once again Billy calls, "One-two, one-two-three . . ."

The number begins. The band's music has never been more infectious. The music is so gleeful that secretaries pour forth from the studio offices to dance and sing along.

Mailboys, payroll clerks, accountants, security guards: the word swiftly spreads that someone is making *amazing* music. Soon the recording studio is packed. B.D. turns on the intercoms throughout the building so that everyone in the huge skyscraper complex can enjoy this triumphant moment. He then turns on the P.A. system outside the building: traffic stops dead; windows open all over Century City; everyone grooves to the joyous, loving sounds of Sgt. Pepper's Lonely Hearts Club Band.

"A perfect take!" announces Easy Mix Jack. "This is the easiest band I've ever recorded."

B.D., Dougie and Lucy lean forward. Their

grins grow broader, their nostrils flare wildly. They drink champagne and they laugh and dream of the money they're going to make.

The album is completed in a mere two hours— a record for a new band. B.D. clutches the platinum-colored, two-inch tape to his heart. "I want this album in the stores tomorrow!" he orders.

Throughout the night, the tape is mixed down, reduced to one-half of an inch in size, mastered and pressed.

By morning there are one million disks ready for national distribution.

All through the night, American D.J.'s—aware that a musical miracle is about to happen—have been phoning B.D. Records begging for the opportunity to debut this mysterious new album.

It is decided to fly the five most important D.J.'s in the country to Hollywood the following morning. There, they will simultaneously debut the album by sharing the opportunity to play it first.

Awakened from their sleep by a phone call from B.D., the D.J.'s rub their eyes, then eagerly accept the invitation.

The next afternoon B.D.'s limousine drives up to Tower Records. The store windows have been plastered with copies of the jacket of the album made by the Lonely Hearts Club Band the night before. Hundreds of adoring new fans scream and yell.

"It's the Lonely Hearts Club Band!"

"Billy, I'm yours!"

"Dave, I'd do anything for you!" they scream.

Dave is being fondled on all sides. He is dragged away and pulled into the record store. He picks up a record. "Look—our album!"

But Bob is way past him. "They're all our record album!"

Billy can't believe it. "All of them?"

Dougie boasts, "Every single album in the store is the debut album of the one, the only Sgt. Pepper's Lonely Hearts Club Band!"

The boys stand next to B.D. They are introduced to the D.J.'s, who drool all over them and act like groupies. Flashbulbs by the hundreds pop to document this meeting of D.J.'s and recording artists.

Then the album is put on a turntable; it begins to play.

At the first sound of it, the girls outside scream and cheer and jump up and down. They knock over a guard and storm the store.

The boys don't know where to turn first. They scurry to the top of the huge stacks of their first album. Then the girls attack. They begin to topple the stacks. Like Tarzan, Bob yells "Ahhhhhh!" as the stacks fall to the floor. They scream with laughter as they look at each other, literally up to their necks in their very first L.P.

By the next day, that album and the boys' first single are the number-one records in America.

B.D. decides the band's first engagement will be at the Roxy Theatre, Los Angeles' premier rock club.

The minute the band is announced, the engagement is sold out. Hundreds of fans camp out for days in front of the Roxy in the hopes of securing a ticket. The tickets are being scalped at upward of one hundred dollars a seat.

Inside, the band is more magical than they've ever been. Dressed simply in T-shirts and jeans, their entrance is greeted by cheers and endless standing ovations. Just as in Heartland, their music drives the audience wild as they rev up and begin to play one of their favorite tunes:

Well, you should see Polythene Pam
She's so good looking but she looks
    like a man

Well, you should see her in drag,
    dressed in her polythene bag,
Yes, you should see Polythene Pam
Yeh, yeh, yeh.

Get a dose of her in jack-boot and
    kilt,
She's killer diller when she's
    dressed to the hilt.

She's the kind of a girl that makes
    the news of the world,
Yes, you could say she was
    attractively built.
Yeh, yeh, yeh

Each night after the gig, fans line the street to catch a glimpse of the boys.

"In the history of rock 'n' roll," reports *Rolling Stone*, "never has there been a debut engagement as thrilling as that of Sgt. Pepper's Lonely Hearts Club Band!"

B.D., thrilled by their success, instantly cancels the boys' tour of small clubs and books them into

New York's Carnegie Hall. The engagement is sold out before a single advertisement is placed.

At the airport the band is greeted by the Mayor of New York. The boys are given a ticker-tape parade down Broadway. All of New York is at their feet.

One number in particular drives the Carnegie Hall audience wild:

> She came in through the bathroom
>   window
> Protected by a silver spoon.
> But now she sucks her thumb and
>   wonders
> By the banks of her own lagoon
>
> Didn't anybody tell her?
> Didn't anybody see?
> Sunday's on the phone to Monday
> Tuesday's on the phone to me
>
> She said she'd always been a
>   dancer
> She worked at fifteen clubs
>   a day
> And though she thought I knew
>   the answer
> Well I knew what I could not
>   say
>
> Didn't anybody tell her?
> Didn't anybody see?
>
> Sunday's on the phone to Monday
> Tuesday's on the phone to me
> Oh, yeah

And so I quit the police department
And got myself a steady job
And though she tried her best
   to help me
She could steal, but she could
   not rob

Didn't anybody tell her?
Didn't anybody see?
Sunday's on the phone to Monday
Tuesday's on the phone to me
Oh, yeah.

B.D. immediately books the boys into the largest arenas in the United States. All concerts are sold out by the end of the day.

Never before has any band had the best-selling album and single in the country and a sold-out arena tour—all in the space of the first week of their professional careers.

Each night a ballad of theirs makes the arena audiences listen with incredible intensity, only to explode in a round of cheers at the end of the song:

He's a real Nowhere Man,
Sitting in his Nowhere Land,
Making all his nowhere plans
   for nobody.
Doesn't have a point of view
Knows not where he's going to
Isn't he a bit like you
   and me?

Nowhere Man, please listen
You don't know what you're
   missing

Nowhere Man, the world is at
  your command

He's as blind as he can be
Just sees what he wants to see
Nowhere Man can you see me
  at all?
Doesn't have a point of view
Knows not where he's going to
Isn't he a bit like you
  and me?

Nowhere Man, don't worry
Take your time, don't hurry
Leave it all till somebody else
  lends you a hand

He's a real Nowhere Man
Sitting in his Nowhere Land
Making all his nowhere plans
  for nobody.
Making all his nowhere plans
  for nobody
Making all his nowhere plans
  for nobody.

Backstage readying for a concert in another
packed arena, Dougie dictates a memo to his new
secretary. "Renée, please see that the helicopter
is on the roof at precisely 12:30 to take us to our
private jet. I don't want the boys accosted again
after the show. It tires them out too much."

Dave interrupts. "Dougie, old boy, I'm not tired,
and I love being attacked by all those ladies!"

Mark and Bob concur. "Yes, let them attack
all they like!" They laugh playfully.

But Lucy interjects as she combs Billy's hair, "No, boys, Dougie's right. Why, Billy, here, is too exhausted for words."

Billy just smiles. He misses Strawberry, but he also loves his new life—a life he never imagined he would ever be having.

Onstage he scans the packed arena. He looks out at his adoring fans. "This song is just for you because I love you!" he shouts.

There is uncontrollable screaming.

"Sing to me, Billy!"

"Mark, show me your chest!"

"You're wonderful, Bob!"

Policemen can't keep the crowds from storming the stage. The screams turn into full-fledged hysteria. Confetti and balloons fly through the air. And the whole crowd stands on chairs, singing, dancing and swaying to the music. This music makes them happy; it makes them feel good; it is powerful enough to keep them young forever! The boys bow; they love the happiness their music brings!

Meanwhile, back in Heartland, Ernest and Saralinda Shears, Bill and Zena Henderson, and Stuart, Linda and Strawberry Fields cluster around a small TV set in the office of the Heartland Home for Our Beloved Aged, watching "The Sgt. Pepper's Lonely Hearts Club Band Special." Leonard Bernstein conducts a two-hundred-piece orchestra. One hundred dancers boogie in front of a large curtain.

Then the curtain parts. Behind it is another curtain. It rises.

And there they are—Sgt. Pepper's Lonely Hearts Club Band. The band is on a hydraulic lift. Slowly they rise into the air, accompanied by roars of approval from the studio audience.

Strawberry's eyes fill with tears. She hugs her mother. "I'm so happy for them," she whispers.

No one says anything else. They are all speechless! Can this really be our boys from Heartland? Are we really their parents? Can this really be happening to us? They all gaze intently at the television screen. The boys sing merrily:

> • • •
> We're Sgt. Pepper's Lonely Hearts
>   Club Band
> We hope you will enjoy the show
> We're Sgt. Pepper's Lonely Hearts
>   Club Band
> Sit back and let the evening go.
> Sgt. Pepper's Lonely, Sgt. Pepper's
>   Lonely, Sgt. Pepper's Lonely Hearts
>   Club Band.
> • • •

In his van, Mustard studies Strawberry. He's getting itchy. When will Central Headquarters send instructions? Isn't it time that he make his move?

A month goes by. The TV set in the Heartland Home for Our Beloved Aged has been replaced by a giant-sized Advent screen. Mr. Kite, the old folks, the silly girls, the brashy boys and many other loyal Heartlanders pack the room. They all stare delightedly at the boys, who have been called back to star in "The Sgt. Pepper's Lonely Hearts Club Band Special II."

Old Lady Pearl sighs, "You turn me on, Billy! You always did! I'm glad I knew you when!"

Saralinda and Ernest, Stuart and Linda, and Bill and Zena look embarrassedly at each other. Weren't they silly to worry about what would happen to their boys when their boys hit the Big Time?

Spotlights bathe the Big Deal Records offices in Century City. B.D. and Lucy pass a bottle of champagne back and forth as they stand on the roof of the building overlooking all of Los Angeles. The city lights twinkle brazenly in the distance.

B.D. reaches over and pulls a switch. The words NUMBER ONE light up between the huge "B" and the huge "D" on top of the building.

"We're number one!" gasps B.D. as he plants his mouth on Lucy's.

"So what's next?" asks Lucy, pulling away.

"Now we'll steal their money!"

Lucy suddenly throws her arms around B.D.'s neck. "I respect your mind," she purrs. "I really do!"

Strawberry lies on her bed staring at the pictures of Billy plastered on every wall. "Billy, I miss you," she sighs. "It's not enough to see you on television. I need to be with you."

Suddenly she becomes alarmed. She looks around. Even though she is alone, she knows she is being watched. She looks around again. Then she scampers under her bed. She is still being watched. She starts to cry uncontrollably.

Mr. Mustard laughs as he watches the tears roll down Strawberry's cheeks. "Someday, my pretty, you'll be thinking only of me!"

Wrapped in a mustard-colored towel, he lies on his mustard-colored massage table. The computerettes work over him, trying to get the tension out of his body.

"Barbra, a little harder on the lower back," he growls.

She presses too hard.

"Not that hard, you boob tube!"

The computerettes talk among themselves as they work on Mr. Mustard.

Barbra continues her rubbing. "What a meanie! He's a mean, mean man!"

Concurs Martha, "And a cheapie, too. Isn't this one the cheapest thing you've ever seen?"

Irma massages his neck. "But he's cute—even if he is getting old!"

A message suddenly appears on the videoscreen. The rubbing stops; everyone stares at the screen. This could be the moment they've all been waiting for.

THE TIME HAS COME!
JUST STEAL THE INSTRUMENTS
IN THE MUSEUM!
AND HEARTLAND WILL BE YOURS!

Mr. Mustard rubs his hands together in gleeful anticipation. "Rub harder, you fools! Tonight I'm going to be king!"

Midnight. Mr. Mustard and Brute quietly tiptoe through the unlocked front door of Heartland Museum. Club in hand, Mr. Kite sits asleep behind his desk.

Brute puts his hand over Mr. Kite's mouth. Mr. Kite bites hard, but he is frail and old. He is quickly bound and gagged.

Mr. Mustard grabs the cornet from the hands

of one of the effigies of Sgt. Pepper's Lonely Hearts Club Band. The cornet blows in protest. It blows and blows and blows.

"Shush!" says Mustard. The cornet is quickly stuffed with a mustard-stained handkerchief and dumped into a large sack.

Brute does his best to unleash the saxophone from the hands of its effigy, but the fingers will not budge.

"Let me do it, you dummy!"

Brute grins. "Right-o, boss."

But Mustard cannot unleash the instrument. He shouts at Brute, "Do something, you boob!"

"Okie-dokie." He breaks the hands off the statue and stuffs the hands and the saxophone into the sack.

Meanwhile, the tuba oom-pah-pahs frantically. And the saxophone tries to climb out of the sack. Mr. Mustard viciously slaps the sax once, then again. He slaps it and slaps it and slaps it until it is too weak to resist anymore.

The bass drum rolls toward the door. Brute chases after it and lunges on top of it.

Mustard thrusts it into the sack too. He ties the sack with a thick rope. Mustard and Brute lug the sack back to the van. The deed is done!

The effigies weep; a bound and gagged Mr. Kite weeps; the Sgt. Pepper weathervane weeps, too.

Heartland sleeps peacefully with no idea of what is about to happen now that Sgt. Pepper's musical instruments are gone!

Mustard has never been happier. He is so happy he makes up a theme song for himself:

Mean Mr. Mustard sleeps in the
    park
Shaves in the dark trying to
    save paper.
Sleeps in a hole in the road
Saving up to buy some clothes
Keeps a ten bob note up his nose

Such a mean old man,
Such a mean old man.

His sister Pam works in a shop
She never stops, she's a go-getter
Takes him out to look at the Queen
Only place that he's ever been
Always shouts out something
    obscene.

Such a dirty old man,
Such a dirty old man.

The very next day, a blazing sun appears. It burns through the day and into the night, drying up the streams and playing havoc with the crops.

The sun blazes all day, every day, for a week. By the week's end, the farmers have been ruined.

Mr. Mustard appears at the doorsteps of their homes. He offers to buy their property. They will sell at a loss, but at least they will have some cash. They will need this cash to start over again somewhere where the sun has not gone mad.

One farmer finally sells, then another, and then a third.

Mustard immediately begins to speculate the land that he has just purchased.

Riff-raff arrives in Heartland. Twenty-four-hour

motels open overnight; slot machines line the streets; beggars roam the gutters. Soon there is litter everywhere and graffiti is scribbled on the walls of the Heartland City Hall:

HEARTLAND SUCKS MUD.

BILLY SHEARS IS UNTRUE.

HEARTLAND EQUALS FILTH.

DOWN WITH HEARTLAND—FOREVER!

Windows are broken; stores are burgled; people are mugged; strange girls prowl around, giving the farmers "the eye."

Postman Hank delivers packages in plain brown wrappers.

And every building in the Heartland town square soon bears a sign:

FORECLOSED BY MUSTARD
REAL ESTATE!

Meanwhile Mustard opens the Mustard Loan Company and the Mustard Quick Money Association. Worst of all, he converts the Heartland bandstand into Mr. Mustard's Greasy Mustard Burger Stand. Suddenly, the landscape of Heartland is dominated by a giant, dripping, greasy Mustard Burger sculpture. The Heartlanders stare at the hideous sight. And then they finally realize they are doomed!

As many of them who can afford it move away.

Mustard surveys his work through his periscope. He watches the Heartlanders leave.

Rena and Librarian Richard slowly carry piles of books to their station wagon. Farmer Jack waves a sorrowful good-bye to Ivy before he steps on the gas and drives his loaded truck away from Heartland forever.

Each departure makes Mustard jump up and down with glee.

Irma, Barbra and Martha slap him on his back. "Hip, hip, hooray!" they cheer. "That's a job well done!"

A message appears on the videoscreen.

KEEP ONE INSTRUMENT FOR YOURSELF.

DELIVER ONE TO DR. MAXWELL EDISON.

DELIVER ONE TO FATHER SUN.

DELIVER ONE TO "FVB."

THESE INSTRUMENTS WILL GIVE US
THE POWER TO RAISE OUR ARMY!

Mustard knows he must follow the instructions to a tee.

Keep one instrument for yourself. Mustard decides to keep the bass drum. The other three instruments are bound and gagged.

Deliver one to Dr. Maxwell Edison. Mustard puts the saxophone into a sack. The saxophone seems the perfect gift for a mad doctor. Mustard laughs. My, how this saxophone would love to wiggle itself free!

Deliver one to Father Sun. Mustard stuffs the cornet into a separate sack. Just the thing for a religious fanatic!

Inside the sack, the cornet begins to swell. It swells until the mustard-colored handkerchief stuffed within it pops out. An anguished cry pierces the night. Mr. Mustard stuffs the handkerchief back into the horn and ties the sack shut.

Mustard puts the tuba into a third sack. All the sacks viciously shake back and forth; they moan terrible groans.

Mustard is elated. A map to the headquarters of "FVB" appears on the videoscreen. Mustard wishes he didn't have to send Brute on this job. Brute could bump into "FVB" and have a cup of tea with him, her, it or them and not ever know the difference! Nevertheless, Brute is the only messenger he has.

Brute picks up the sacks and sets out to deliver the instruments. He climbs up on a small mustard-colored moped.

Mustard stands in the doorway of the van. "And don't make any mistakes, dumbbell!" he shrieks at Brute.

Brute grins dopily. "Yes, indeedy," he says as he pulls away.

Mustard wonders if Brute had been punched enough before he had been sent on his way.

From the van, Mustard gazes out at Heartland. Soon its name will be Mustardville. Mustard is a winner. Still, memories of his loser status flash through his mind.

One day, he remembers, he was at the desk of his tacky real estate office in downtown Duluth when a smiling, thin little girl wearing a brown shirt and brown shorts had knocked on his door.

"Good afternoon, Mr. Mustard. I'm here to make your life better. All you need to do is take our free personality test," she had said in a cordial, yet impersonal tone.

Since he had had no customers in some time— four months, to be precise—he had replied, "Sure, sure. Anything to pass the time of day."

He had passed the test—with flying colors— scoring a perfect score in the *loser* category.

Then the little girl told him that he could finally become a winner! He merely had to commit his money, mind and life to the coded messages that would appear on the videoscreens that would soon be installed in his home, his office and his van.

Thought Mustard: Could I be more of a loser than I am? No! So I'll try anything!

And he did!

And now he had his own *town*! He stares at Heartland once again.

Strawberry stands on the porch of the Heartland Home for Our Beloved Aged.

Suddenly the computerettes signal Mustard. He steps into the van. On the videoscreen appears the legend:

WE HATE LOVE.

WE HATE JOY.

WE LOVE MONEY.

REMEMBER, LOSERS CAN BE WINNERS!

Mustard and the computerettes salute proudly. The videoscreen has never lied to them.

Strawberry stares out at her devastated homeland.

Old Lady Pearl swings on the porch's rocker. "All you do is stand around all day. Do something useful. Get out of here!" she snaps.

Everyone in Heartland has been affected by the horrible changes.

Strawberry politely ignores Old Lady Pearl. She walks down the steps toward the bandstand.

Mrs. Fields calls after her. "Just where do you think you're going? This place is filthy! Scrub down the walls! Do them now! Then sweep the sidewalk! Then take out the garbage! Then change the sheets . . . !"

Strawberry continues walking. She is tired of everyone's abuse, tired of cleaning walls only to find them filthy the next morning, tired of living in a nightmare, tired of missing Billy.

The town square is filled with beggars, each of them shrieking for just enough money for a cup of coffee . . . enough money to find a place to sleep . . . enough money to buy a bus ticket and get out of this godforsaken place.

Strawberry gets closer to the bandstand. With each step she takes, she is simultaneously brushed against, cursed at and pinched.

She screams out loud! But nobody cares! "Billy, come home!" she calls as her eyes search the town square for help. Someone has climbed on top of Heartland City Hall and mercilessly bent the Sgt. Pepper weathervane out of shape.

The weathervane weeps; so does she.

Mustard lies in the van, peacefully snoring away the night. The computerettes watch Strawberry through the periscope, as they have been dutifully programmed to do.

*   *   *

At Yankee Stadium, the Sgt. Pepper Lonely Hearts Club Band waits backstage as hundreds of thousands of fans take their seats.

Lucy drapes her arms around Billy's neck. "Sing one just for me, honey," she teases. Laughing, she then gives him a playful bite on the neck.

Billy laughs too. "Watch that, or I'll never make it to the stage." He takes her into his arms. They dissolve into a kiss.

Just before dawn, Strawberry throws open her bedroom window. She has spent the whole night sitting up in bed staring at the pictures of Billy that adorn the walls of her bedroom. The air is filled with thick, sulphurous smoke. She looks down at the streets. They are lined with beer cans, cigarette butts and turned-over garbage cans. Drunks sleep in the gutter. The town looks and smells like a garbage dump.

Strawberry gets up, quickly dresses and packs a valise. She scribbles a note to her parents. Then she tiptoes down the stairs and she's out the door.

Still in their nightclothes, Mr. and Mrs. Fields read the note:

Dear Mom and Dad,

   I've got to leave you for a little while. Please try and understand.

                                        I love you,
                                        Strawberry

Stuart Fields sits quietly at his desk. "I don't understand that girl. I just don't understand her!"

Linda Fields nods. "I was always here when she needed me!"

They clutch each other tightly. "How could she leave us?"

Strawberry waits at the Heartland Bus Depot for the Heartland–Los Angeles bus. She turns to look back. There is a huge, sooty, black cloud hovering over all of Heartland!

The bus pulls up. Without looking back, she hops onto it. And she's gone!

SEVEN

The computerettes stare at Strawberry. They know she's leaving. Together they sing to Mustard, but he is lost in deep sleep. The computerettes sing louder, then louder, then louder:

Wednesday morning at five o'clock
   as the day begins . . .
Silently closing her bedroom door
Leaving the note that she hoped
   would say more
She goes downstairs to the kitchen
   clutching her handkerchief
Quietly turning the back door key
Stepping outside she is free
She . . . is leaving . . . home.

She (We gave her most of our lives)
Is leaving (Sacrificed most of our
   lives)
Home (We gave her everything
   money could buy)

She's leaving home after living
   alone
For so many years.
Bye, bye.

Father snores as his wife gets
   into her dressing gown.
Picks up the letter that's lying
   there
Standing alone at the top of the
   stairs
She breaks down and cries to her
   husband
Daddy, our baby's gone.
Why would she treat us so
   thoughtlessly
How could she do this to me?
She . . . is leaving . . . home.
. . .

The computerettes know their duty; they must wake up Mustard.

Sulks Barbra, "Do we have to wake him up? If he catches her, we'll never get him back!"

Irma agrees. "Let him sleep! He'll get over her!"

Martha scolds, "Are you both crazy? He'll turn us into transistor radios if we let him down! We must get him up somehow!"

They all think for a long, hard moment. *Singing won't do it. Maybe static will.* They all put themselves on "current overload" and begin to crackle, whelp and hum.

Still it doesn't work. Timidly, in desperation, Martha raps Mustard on the head with her wire arm. "Mustard, honey, I think you just might want to wake up! Have we got news for you!"

In a final effort to wake him up, Martha douses him with a pail of water.

"What is going on here?" Mustard roars as he pops up and shakes himself off.

The computerettes nonchalantly point to the videoscreen. They press the "Replay" button. Mustard watches Strawberry hopping onto the Heartland–Los Angeles bus.

The bus pulls past Mustard's van. Mustard is frantic. He bangs against the cab door. "Wake up in there and follow that bus!" he screams.

Brute doesn't understand. But he starts up the van anyway. Mustard glowers. Can't Brute do anything right? He had been to the lair of "FVB" and all he could report back was that the music was too loud.

"Idiot! Idiot! Idiot!" Mustard fumes.

Strawberry huddles in a corner of the bus. She is cold, hungry and tired. Exhausted from lack of sleep, she tries to close her eyes, but the gruff gentleman in the seat next to her has other ideas.

"Hey, baby-doll," he says. "Wanna make small talk?"

"No, thank you," replies the tired Strawberry.

"But it's cold in here." The man puts his arms around her. "What say we keep warm together!"

Strawberry gets up and changes her seat.

"You're a prude!" barks the stranger.

The band finishes a rousing number and leaves the stage. Lucy mops Billy's brow. "You're real good to me," he says gently.

"I can get better!" she replies lustily.

*   *   *

Strawberry tries to swallow the food served on the bus, but she loses her appetite when she sees crawlies on the cranberries.

Babies cry all through the day and night. The bus develops a foul smell. Strawberry is ready to give up . . . but then what?

The only thing that keeps her going is the small picture she carries of Billy. She touches the picture and closes her eyes as she tries to shut out the awful world.

The van has a flat tire. Mustard fumes in the back while Brute changes it.

"It's finished, boss," Brute replies. He climbs back into the cab and tries to start up the van, but he has no luck. He has changed the wrong tire!

Mustard sneaks up behind him and starts to pummel him with a wrench.

"I want that girl!" he hisses. "We've got to get moving!"

He hits Brute over the head with the wrench, and the wrench breaks in two.

Brute smiles. "Thanks, your honor, sir."

The Heartland–Los Angeles bus finally reaches its destination. It slowly fights its way down Sunset Strip and pulls to a stop in front of the Continental Hyatt House. A relieved Strawberry gets off. She walks down Sunset Boulevard. Hundreds line the street waiting to get into such clubs as the Roxy, Rainbow, Whiskey, Gazzaris and Pat Collins's Celebrity Club. The parking lot between the Roxy and Rainbow is packed with girls dressed like boys and boys dressed like girls.

A couple of bikers at the curb look her over.

"Hey, Mama, say what?"

"Is this one for real? She looks like something out of *Hansel and Greaseball!*"

They laugh. Strawberry nervously walks on.

"Don't ignore me, Mama," they call after her. "We'd like a fairy tale of our own."

Strawberry feels faint.

She has never seen so many cars, so many people. The smog chokes her; the noise deafens her. The street throbs with the dull roar of endless traffic. She notices for the first time that above the street are a giant series of billboards.

She looks up at them.

They look down at her.

One, in particular, catches her eye:

LUCY AND THE DIAMONDS ON
B.D. RECORDS—THE TRASHIEST
ACT EVER!

Strawberry literally can hear music pouring forth from the billboard.

Picture yourself in a boat on a
    river
With tangerine trees and marmalade
    skies
Somebody calls you, you answer
    quite slowly
A girl with kaleidoscope eyes.

Cellophane flowers of yellow and
    green
Towering over your head

Look for the girl with the sun
    in her eyes
And she's gone!

Lucy in the sky with diamonds.
Lucy in the sky with diamonds.
Lucy in the sky with diamonds, ah.

Follow her down to a bridge by
    a fountain
Where rocking horse people eat
    marshmallow pies,
Everyone smiles as you drift
    past the flowers
That grow so incredibly high.
Newspaper taxis appear on the shore
Waiting to take you away
Climb in the back with your head
    in the clouds
And you're gone.

Lucy in the sky with diamonds.
Lucy in the sky with diamonds.
Lucy in the sky with diamonds, ah.

Picture yourself on a train in
    a station
With plasticine porters with
    looking-glass ties
Suddenly someone is there at the
    turnstile.
The girl with kaleidoscope eyes.

Lucy in the sky with diamonds.
Lucy in the sky with diamonds.
Lucy in the sky with diamonds, ah!!
Lucy in the sky with diamonds, ah!!

She stares at the billboard. Suddenly, it comes to life. Is she imagining it? Is she going mad?

Lucy towers above her. She looks down at Strawberry. She bumps and grinds, shimmies to and fro, then sticks out her tongue and laughs wildly.

What kind of woman is this? Can this be what the world is all about?

Lucy points to the billboard across the street. Strawberry turns her head. It's Sgt. Pepper's Lonely Hearts Club Band!

Lucy reaches out across the street to Billy. And then Billy comes alive! Strawberry gasps.

"Billy! Billy!" she calls.

People look at her as they drive past in their cars.

"Nut job!" one screams. But Strawberry can't take her eyes off the living billboards.

One girl giggles. "I don't blame her; I'm crazy about Billy, too!"

Strawberry, Billy and Lucy hungrily reach out for each other. Begging and taunting! Pleading and enticing! And then Billy jumps across Sunset Boulevard to join Lucy. He throws his arms around her. And both billboards evaporate in two tremendous puffs of red-hot steam.

Strawberry faints at the sight.

EIGHT

Oh, darling, please believe me
I'll never do you no harm
Believe me when I tell you
I'll never do you no harm.
Oh, darling.
If you leave me
I'll never make it alone
Believe me when I beg you
Don't ever leave me alone.
When you told me—you didn't
   need me anymore
Well you know, I nearly broke
   down and cried.
When you told me you didn't
   need me anymore
Well you know I nearly broke
   down and died.
Oh, darling, if you leave me
I'll never make it alone
Believe me when I tell you
I'll never do you no harm.

Sgt. Pepper's Lonely Hearts Club Band is busy cutting a new single called "Oh, Darling" in B.D.'s Century City recording studio. B.D., Dougie and Lucy sit in the control booth. They take turns swigging champagne and gobbling down caviar canapés.

Dougie brushes his hand against Lucy's bare back. She pulls away. "Not while Billy's singing," she whispers. Then she adds, "Whenever Billy's around, you don't stand a chance, chump!"

"Come on," Dougie snaps.

"Will you shut up, punk!" B.D. orders. "You're interfering with the tapping of my magic fingers!"

A squad car pulls up to the Century City Towers. "I hope you feel better, ma'am," the police captain says paternally as he ushers Strawberry from the car. "Next time, don't take such a long bus ride on such an empty stomach."

"Thank you, Captain. You've been very kind."

"This is the address you've been looking for. Now, don't get into trouble, and good luck."

The Captain steps back into his car and pulls away.

Strawberry stares up at the huge "B" and huge "D." They scare her.

Slowly, she makes her way toward the ominous-looking skyscraper. She walks into the building. The night watchman looks her over. "The band is in the recording studio," he says matter-of-factly. "Press 'Basement.'"

Strawberry steps into the elevator and does as she was told. The elevator heads downward. The doors open and she walks into the studio and stands in the shadows. Billy is singing! He's there!

She has finally found him. She breathes a sigh of relief!

"I love you, Billy Shears!" She mouths the words silently so that she does not disturb the session.

Billy spots her first. He can hardly believe his eyes. He flies out of the studio into the control booth and scoops her into his arms. "Strawberry! Strawberry! Strawberry!" He covers her with a hundred small kisses.

She starts to weep hysterically. She is so happy to be with him, so happy that he still loves her, so happy to be here!

"Billy, I missed you! I couldn't stay away any longer! I hope you're not angry."

"Are you crazy? Every song I sing is for you." Billy doesn't stop kissing her.

Lucy stares at the pair. She is furious. "Whoever is she? I'll dismember her!" she says to no one in particular.

The young lovers hold each other tightly.

Mark, Dave and Bob pick up their mikes and press their faces against the glass that separates them from the control booth. With great merriment, they serenade Strawberry. She runs to the glass and kisses their faces.

Billy starts kissing her again. He is in no mood to share her with anyone. "Tell me you're staying! Tell me you'll stay with me!"

Once again, she becomes hysterical.

"Strawberry, I want you to stay!"

"Billy, about Heartland—Heartland is dead!" She blurts out the words in one agonizing breath.

Billy gasps. "What did you say?"

Strawberry sobs as she tells the tale. She describes the theft of Sgt. Pepper's instruments, the arrival of Mr. Mustard, and Heartland's transformation into a garbage dump. "Help us! Please help us, Billy!" she moans.

Billy is ashen-faced. He buries his head in his hands.

Suddenly Strawberry begins to scream uncontrollably. "He's here! Save me! He's here! I know it!"

"Who's here?"

"Mr. Mustard. He never stops looking at me. I can feel his eyes burning holes in me! He's here someplace! I know he's here!"

Strawberry runs to the window. Mustard's van is parked outside.

Billy dashes into the studio. Quickly he tells Mark, Dave and Bob what has happened.

"Don't worry, Strawberry, we'll get him!" assures Mark. "And we'll save Heartland, too!"

Bob puffs out his chest. "No one is going to ruin Heartland—not while I'm around!"

Dave flexes his muscles. "One for all and all for one! Together we'll save the town we love!"

The boys dash from the studio determined to give Mr. Mustard exactly what he deserves!

B.D. punches Dougie in the arm. "I don't know what's going on, dunce, but I think it's trouble! Go after them before we lose our gravy train!"

Dougie, Lucy and B.D. follow the boys into the street.

Mr. Mustard and Brute stand on the sidewalk staring at the huge "B" and the huge "D." Suddenly they spot the boys and Strawberry dashing from the building. Mustard and Brute stare at the boys; the boys stare back at them.

Mustard socks Brute in the nose. "Get them, you dummy! Render them useless!"

Brute dives for Billy as Mr. Mustard attempts

to hide in the van. But Billy dives beneath Brute's legs, grabs Mustard and jumps on top of him. Brute pulls Billy off Mustard and lifts him high into the air. He is about to pound him to the ground when Mark, Dave and Bob jump on him.

Brute continues to throttle Billy as he fights off the Henderson brothers. With a few swift blows, Mark, Dave and Bob are wounded and bleeding. Then Brute once again lifts Billy into the air—this time he will destroy him for good! Billy gasps. He is sure the end is in sight. Brute lifts him higher. As he does, the guitar slung over Billy's shoulder rubs against the buttons on Brute's clothes. A series of dazzling chords emerges from this combination of guitar strings and buttons. Brute swoons. He rubs Billy up and down against his body. The sound is magical. He rubs Billy even harder and harder and harder.

The boys immediately catch on. They lift their battered and bruised bodies and begin to sing to Brute.

Brute gently puts Billy down and starts to waltz with Mustard. Mustard jumps on Brute's toes. "Stop it! Get them! Get them!" he shrieks.

But now mighty Brute is charging through fields of clover looking for the Brutess of his dreams.

Everyone edges toward the van, singing and playing all the while. Suddenly, they are in it. They zoom off into the night.

Mustard watches his van disappear. "This is war!" he gasps. He pulls at his hair.

A taxi drives by and Mustard hails it. He jumps in, then jumps out, grabs Brute and jumps in once again. "Follow my van!" he rasps.

B.D., Lucy and Dougie watch from the curb. They are thoroughly confused. Who is this strange-smelling, peculiar-looking man, and why has the band stolen his van?

"Don't worry!" says Dougie. Billy's gone. Now he can look after Lucy. He reaches out and attempts to put his arm around the wild-eyed knock-out.

"Who are you kidding?" Lucy snaps as she removes Dougie's hand from her. "You're *nothing*—that's what you are!" Lucy starts to saunter away down the street.

Suddenly she turns and says, "If you jerks can't get this band back, I'm through with the both of you!" Then she continues on her way.

"If you don't get this band back, you're through —forever!" B.D. barks at Dougie. Then he turns his head and starts walking back to his building.

Dougie stands alone on the sidewalk. He'll think of something! He has to! But what?

A small truck pulls up. "Organic yogurt with sprouts and honey?" offers a smiling, long-haired youth driving the truck.

"Drop dead!" Dougie growls. "I don't want health—I want wealth!"

Irma, Barbra and Martha can't believe their wire eyes. These boys are much cuter than Mustard and Brute! There's Billy . . . and Mark . . . and Bob . . . and that one driving the van, Dave. And then there's also that blonde thing over there that Mustard is so ga-ga over. But there's only one of her, and all these male cuties! This is the peachiest surprise they've ever stored in their computer memory banks.

Barbra coos as she wraps her wire arms around Mark. "Honey, you can turn on my transistors anytime."

Martha mothers Bob. "Now, honey, just put your feet here, and I'll bring you a glass of milk."

Irma can't even talk. She is so excited that her tubes keep lighting up at random intervals.

Billy whispers tenderly, "Irma, you have the brightest eyes," as he gazes lovingly at her bulbs.

Barbra pushes Mark away. "Hey, there, I want some of that sweet talk, too! My eyes are just as bright as Irma's!"

Irma protectively wraps her arms around Billy and Mark. "These are mine!"

Barbra pushes Irma away. "Why should you have two? Share and share alike."

Billy rubs Martha's neck. Mark tickles her feet as he whispers sweet nothings. "Sweet Martha . . ."

Barbra scolds him. "We've only reached the blush stage. Martha is much more impressionable, so don't turn her on!"

Martha giggles. "Yeah, I become uncontrollable!"

The boys instantly cluster around Martha. They kiss and caress her while they whisper sweet nothings in her ear.

Martha laughs violently. "Stop it!" she moans.

Billy tickles her neck. "Please, Martha, we have to know where the instruments are!"

Martha begins: "Dr. Maxwell's . . ."

Barbra pushes Billy away. "Martha, no!"

Irma grabs Mark's arm. "It's not fair!"

But Martha can't be stopped. She's in ecstasy. She screams out, "Dr. Maxwell's Institute of Youth!"

Billy finds a phonebook and looks up the address.

The van speeds into the night. But now, instead of sneaking through streets, it rides with a sense of pride; after all, it is carrying the boys from Heartland!

Irma, Barbra and Martha sit on the boys' laps and croon electronic ditties to them. But that only makes the boys apprehensive. Dave is pensive. "Do you think Dr. Maxwell's as crazy as Mustard?"

Irma laughs. "Crazier!"

Heartland has been taken over by a strange man who smells of mustard and travels with a giant and three female singing computers in a van from Never-Never Land. And their instruments are at crazy Dr. Maxwell's Institute of Youth. What does it all mean?

Suddenly, the videoscreen lights up:

WE HATE LOVE.

WE HATE JOY.

WE LOVE MONEY.

REMEMBER, LOSERS CAN BE WINNERS!

A sun symbol then appears on the screen. In the center are the initials "FVB."

The computerettes get up and salute the screen —good soldiers each and every one.

Billy sighs, "How can you be loyal to such an evil code?"

"But it's the boss," replies Martha.

"Who is?" asks Billy.

Barbra jumps up and down. "Martha, shut your mouth! You've told enough!"

Martha is confused. "But we don't even know who he is."

The boys look at each other in despair. *Who is responsible for this nightmare?*

NINE

Dr. Maxwell Edison is flanked by a small chorus of surgically attired cuties, each of whom wears the shortest of all possible smocks. This doctor doesn't look much like a doctor. He's too goofy looking. His eyes are crossed; he's got large buck teeth; he's got a crazy grin. Nevertheless, he's dressed in a glittering, glamorous surgeon's gown and wears a huge surgeon's light on top of his head. He also carries a huge silver hammer that glistens in the light.

In the center of his office is his valueless collection of cordless telephones and dead picture tubes. What a devoted collector he is!

Resting on Maxwell's desk is a peculiar battered saxophone. Maxwell smothers it with kisses. "Mmm . . . I love you!" This saxophone has been given to him by "FVB," and it has suddenly made him rich!

Once he had been a lowly doctor who preferred

to kill rather than heal. "Why prescribe aspirin when you can just do 'em in?"

Most people thought Maxwell was nuts, and with good reason. But Maxwell thought he was a progressive. He had told the American Medical Association that the best medicine was no medicine. "Let 'em die. After all, there are so many to replace them with!"

Needless to say, Maxwell's ideas did not make him popular. He had no patients at all.

Then this young girl knocked on his door. She gave him a personality test. He scored one hundred percent in the "loser" category. He had no career and nobody loved him. The girl offered him an opportunity for success, love and lots of money. He was quick to sign up with "FVB" and had allowed a video monitor to be installed in his office.

Now the monitor had told him a magical saxophone was on its way. When it arrived, Dr. Maxwell Edison was suddenly the renowned leader of the Maxwell Institute of Youth. No more would he kill. "Oh, well," he sighed.

Instead, he now had a silver hammer that made old people *young* again! "Clever; very clever."

The videoscreen in Maxwell's office had advised Maxwell to charge five hundred thousand dollars for the transformation to be split equally between him and "FVB." Maxwell heartily agreed. Half was always better than none. "Let's see, two hundred fifty thousand dollars times two hundred patients a day . . ."

Now, day and night, into his office came a parade of the elderly, each carrying a five hundred thousand dollar bill.

Their faces were pinched; their mouths were lined with wrinkles; their eyes were filled with bitterness; and they all wanted to be young again.

To ensure Maxwellian efficiency, Maxwell co-ordinated their smocks: those in green were "OLD AND UGLY"; those in yellow "OLD AND CORRUPT"; those in purple "OLD AND GREEDY"; and those in puce "OLD AND VENAL." All were old and losers.

Maxwell admired the logic of "FVB." After all, the only old people who had the money for this transformation were old monsters. With this transformation, they became young monsters, obviously, and "FVB" wanted as many young monsters as Maxwell could create.

And Maxwell couldn't get them in and out fast enough.

Maxwell didn't know what "FVB" did with the young monsters after he had created them. But who cared?

He loved the money and would do anything to get it—no matter the consequence. Today he's already made eight million dollars! And it's only ten past noon! He had to giggle. This was an easy way to get rich—easier than selling frozen yogurt!

In the van, Dave sits in deep thought. "We could all rush in, grab the instruments, and run out!"

That worries Billy. "It sounds too easy!"

Bob pops up excitely. "We could run in and yell 'Fire, fire!' And then everyone would run out and we could run back in and grab the instruments."

Dave likes that one. "That sounds great!"

"No, no," replies Billy. "They're sure to carry the instruments out with them."

Mark jumps up. "Let's just tell him that he's got our instruments, and if he doesn't turn them over to us we'll send the entire town of Heartland to get them—what's left of Heartland, at any rate."

Billy is always one step ahead. "No, we don't want to warn him. He might disappear."

Bob boasts, "Maybe we should sing as we march in. They might be as crazy as that giant we subdued."

Billy replies, "It's possible. Even if they're not overcome by our sound, we could always use some new fans."

Everyone laughs. But no one knows what will happen when they get to the Maxwell Institute of Youth.

The old people stand in line. Nurse Renée collects the five hundred thousand dollar bills and puts them in a shopping cart. Then Maxwell spits on his hammer and hammers them, one by one. Zap! A shriveled, mean old thing is young again! Maxwell shimmies and shakes. He loves turning rotten old people into rotten young ones. It makes him feel reborn. With each hammering, his laugh grows wilder. What makes him laugh most of all is his money-laden shopping cart.

"Look at that beautiful money!" he gasps. "Don't you just love it!" He looks lovingly at the money, grins crazily, and merrily picks up his hammer once again.

Suddenly he begins to sing and dance:

Joan was quizzical
Studies pataphysical science in
the home
Late nights all alone with a test
tube
Oh, oh, oh, oh
Maxwell Edison
Majoring in medicine calls her on
the phone
"Can I take you out to the pictures,
Jo-o-o-an?"
But as she's getting ready to go
A knock comes on the door
Bang! Bang! Maxwell's Silver
Hammer came down
Upon her head
Clang! Clang! Maxwell's Silver
Hammer made sure
That she was dead.

Back in school again Maxwell
plays the fool again
Teacher gets annoyed
Wishing to avoid an unpleasant
scene
She tells Max to stay when the
class has gone away
So he waits behind
Writing fifty times, "I must not
be so-o-o-o"
But when she turns her back on
the boy
He creeps up from behind
Bang! Bang! Maxwell's Silver
Hammer came down

Upon her head
Clang! Clang! Maxwell's Silver
Hammer made sure
That she was dead.

P.C. Thirty One said, "We've cot a
    dirty one"
Maxwell stands alone
Painting testimonial pictures
Oh, oh, oh, oh
Rose and Valerie screaming from
    the gallery
Say he must go free
The judge does not agree and he
    tells them so-o-o-o
But, as the words are leaving
    his lips
A noise comes from behind
Bang! Bang! Maxwell's Silver
Hammer
Came down upon his head
Clang! Clang! Maxwell's Silver
Hammer made sure
That he was dead.
Silver Hammer

Bang! Bang! Maxwell's Silver
Hammer
Came down upon his head
Clang! Clang! Maxwell's Silver
Hammer made sure
That he was dead!

"Where is your money?" Nurse Renée demands
of some newcomers.

The lead newcomer, an old codger if ever there

was one, replies, "In my pocket—where it belongs!" He grabs the shopping cart and makes a dash for it.

Everyone is distracted by this spry old man.

Disguised as ancients, with white powder in their hair, Silly-Putty wrinkles, hospital gowns and orthopedic shoes, Billy, Mark and Dave suddenly surround the disarmed doctor as Strawberry grabs the saxophone and Bob continues his decoy work with the shopping cart of money.

Maxwell screams and stamps his foot. He will never be a loser again! "Who are these fistfighting octogenarians?" he asks out loud. Then he summons help.

Nurse Rita, Nurse Ivy and Nurse Myrna descend on Mark, Dave and Bob. Blue-belts in karate, they use every move they ever learned as they hammer and throttle the brave lads.

Maxwell grabs a silver hammer. "I'll break your head! I always said killing was better!" he shrieks as he heads straight for Billy. Billy grabs another hammer. A fight to the death has begun!

Billy jumps onto an operating table and kicks Maxwell in the jaw. Maxwell falls backward. Billy grabs Maxwell's hammer. Now he has two. He pounds the doctor with one and Maxwell is suddenly twelve. He pounds him with the other. Maxwell suddenly becomes eight.

The child Maxwell suddenly jumps up. He carries two miniature hammers. He waves them in Billy's face. They instantly paralyze Billy. With all his might, the child Maxwell then slowly picks up a huge silver hammer. With an amazing amount of superhuman strength, he tries to hit Billy over the head with it.

Mark, Dave and Bob grab the child Maxwell

from behind. Mark is kicked in the shin; Dave is given a fierce bite; but Bob pins the child Maxwell to the floor.

"I'll bite you to death!" screams Maxwell. He then bursts into the worst eight-year-old temper tantrum in recorded history. "I won't be a loser!" he swears as angry tears roll down his swollen, little red face. "I won't be a kid loser! I couldn't go through it again!"

"I've got the saxophone!" says Strawberry triumphantly.

"Let's go!" says Billy.

The child Maxwell chases after them, ripping at their clothes and biting them on the arm as they go.

Only when they reach the van do they realize that they have retrieved only one of the four instruments. There are three more to get back. Where are those three? They must know now!

The boys turn to Martha. They coo in her transmitter ears. This time, however, Martha does not respond.

"We have reprogrammed her!" Barbra boasts. "You'll never get a response!"

Martha looks pleadingly at Billy. She'd love to help, but now she can't.

Mark nuzzles Irma's neck. Irma tries not to respond. Each boy masters his charm. These computerettes must be made to help.

If the truth be told, it doesn't take that much. Irma is fed up with those creepy, crawly, bad guys, especially when these kids have such hot-cha sex appeal. "I mustn't," she sighs.

Mark whispers to her, "I'll oil your shoulders if you help us!"

Suddenly, Irma beeps helplessly. "Try the Temple of Electronic Cosmology!"

"The Temple of Electronic Cosmology?"

The boys steel themselves. *The Temple of Electronic Cosmology!* The streets of Los Angeles are filled with disciples of this evil church. These disciples are all young; they all wear brown shorts and brown shirts; their eyes look like empty, burned-out sockets.

The boys are shocked. Who would give Sgt. Pepper's instruments to such bizarre fiends as the rulers of the Temple of Electronic Cosmology?

"The instruments bring happiness," Billy says softly. "What could they possibly want with them?"

The boys know that before too long they'll have their answer. *The Temple of Electronic Cosmology!* A place where young people are turned into the living dead!

TEN

A master session at the Temple of Electronic Cosmology is in progress: a class for all the corrupt old people hammered into youthfulness by Dr. Maxwell. These young losers must now be brainwashed to serve "FVB."

Their eyes are glazed; their mouths are open; their posture is erect as they sit at little school desks in the giant, desolate, gray hall. They all look up at the three giant, swirling television screens hanging before them.

Over and over again, they chant along with the message:

WE HATE LOVE.

WE HATE JOY.

WE LOVE MONEY.

Their chanting echoes throughout the great hall. In never-ending waves of reverberation, the sound bounces from wall to wall until the group is caught up in a giant billboard game of sound.

Suddenly, Father Sun, leader of the Temple, simultaneously appears on the three giant screens. He is dressed in a huge billowing cape. A large, vivid sun is painted on its back. From it are projected hypnotic rays, powerful enough to hypnotize anybody! Music always accompanies the visual display.

Because the world is round, it
   turns me on
Because the world is round
Ah.
Because the wind is high, it
   blows my mind
Because the wind is high
Ah.
Love is old, love is new
Love is all, love is you
Because the sky is blue,
   it makes me cry
Because the sky is blue
Ah.
Love is old, love is new
Love is all, love is you.
Because the sky is blue
   it makes me cry
Because the sky is blue
Ah.

A strong, imposing voice booms over the thirty-two-track Dolby sound system: "You are all open wounds—begging to be healed. I will heal you! You have problems that have immobilized you. I will make them vanish! You are all lower than the earth. I will elevate you to the height of the sun! Repeat after me: 'You are the Father Sun—and we love you!' "

The words appear on the screen. So does a bouncing ball. The disciples follow the ball as it bounces across the screen:

> You-are-the-Father-Sun-and-we-love-you!
> You-are-the-Father-Sun-and-we-love-you!
> You-are-the-Father-Sun-and-we-love-you!
> You-are-the-Father-Sun-and-we-love-you!

Father Sun grins madly. Who would have believed that just last month he had been a loser? Mervin Sun's high school graduating class had included L. Ron Hubbard and Werner Erhard. And they succeeded, but not he!

All his friends had said to him, "Mervin, let's face it, you just don't have the smarts. You're greedy enough, but you don't have the charisma. Who would want to follow you? You'll never be a consciousness hero like the others! Pick another profession! You'd make a terrific school-crossing guard!"

Then that little girl had knocked on his door (you remember her). She had given him a personality test and signed him up after he had scored a perfect score in the "loser" category. He had no career; nobody loved him—you know the story. So he allowed "FVB" to install a video monitor in his empty Temple.

Then a beat-up cornet had arrived, and now the Temple was jammed.

Father Sun knew that he was brainwashing a youth army for "FVB." But who cared? "FVB's" youth troops were "FVB's" business! He was getting rich! And he had followers—hundreds of them. Now his followers had followers of their own. And every day hundreds more arrived. . . . And Mervin was getting richer and richer and richer.

Billy, Mark, Dave, Bob and Strawberry sit in the back of the great hall. They wear brown shorts and brown shirts. They chant: "We hate love. We hate joy. We love money."

Father Sun's voice once again booms over the sound system: "And now you shall stand and pay homage to me. Rise! Rise! Rise, now!" The disciples dutifully stand up and come forth. "Come and display your love and goodwill!"

The disciples march forward. They empty their pockets into giant fishbowls under the videoscreens.

Billy, Mark, Dave, Bob and Strawberry head toward the screens.

The voice continues: "Rise! Rise! And pay homage! You are fools, and I am your master!"

Billy reaches the screens. He grabs a plug, Strawberry another, Mark a third. . . . They pull the plugs. The screens suddenly go blank.

Then they grab the bottoms of the screens; the screens fly up; a surprised Father Sun sits at a desk behind the center screen.

Without his sun cape and platform shoes, Mervin is a balding runt dressed in plaid checked pants and a T-shirt that says RIPOFF.

On his desk is a portable television set tuned to a football game. He slugs a can of beer and belches.

Two young, voluptuous girls sit on his lap. Each holds a calculator. They busy themselves counting the day's profits.

The disciples are astonished. Is this loser Father Sun? Is this loser the one to lead them? Impossible! "No!" they shout. "This can't be true! You are no god; you are a toad!" These angry clones start marching toward Father Sun.

Billy spots Sgt. Pepper's cornet lying on a beanbag chair. He heads directly for it.

The disciples continue on their way. As they go, they stuff their pockets with Father Sun's money. "Ripoff, we'll rip you off!" they chant over and over again.

"Stop it! You are my slaves! I am your father—Father Sun!" Mervin screams feebly. His knees are knocking; his teeth are chattering. He is a sissy! How does a sissy quell a consciousness riot? He tries again: "I am Father Sun! You love me!"

The disciples continue their march. They stop only to scoop up more money.

"Stop it! You're out of control! You're stealing my money!" Sun screams. He tries to turn knobs on the video equipment. " 'FVB,' help me!" he begs. "Help me! Because I need it now!"

The disciples grab the three huge screens and rip them from the ceiling. They throw the school desks in the air and laugh as they smash to the floor. They take Father Sun's desk and smash it to smithereens. They rip and tear and smash and burn and reduce the Temple to a pile of rubble.

Sun lays unconscious on the floor.

"This was no god, just another loser," the disciples chant. They march from the Temple onto Hollywood Boulevard. They then head north and climb the hills. There they set out to demolish the monumental HOLLYWOOD sign.

Inside the Temple, Billy is nowhere to be found.

A frantic search begins. Strawberry calls out, "Billy, please, can you hear me?"

There is no reply.

Mark, Dave and Bob go through the rubble. They lift, pull, push and tear at the battered desks, screens and video equipment. Billy is nowhere.

Mark turns white. "Do you think they've kidnapped him?"

Dave shakes his head. "No, all they wanted was the money!"

"I know he's here! Please don't give up!" begs Strawberry.

They survey the room. Nothing is left undamaged. Everything has been destroyed. It will take days to go through all the rubble. But, once again, the boys dive in.

Suddenly they hear a musical note. It seems to be crying out, "Help!"

Dave yells, "It's the cornet!"

There is another note. They follow the sound.

Suddenly, Mark spies the Sgt. Pepper cornet under one of the giant screens. He is dumbstruck. "It's Billy!"

Mark, Dave, Bob and Strawberry quickly lift the giant screen. A bleeding Billy lies on the floor, and his arms are wrapped tightly around Sgt. Pepper's cornet.

Mark and Dave carry Billy through the rubble to the van. He is covered with gashes and bruises and hardly breathes at all.

Strawberry cuddles Billy in her arms. She whispers gentle remembrances of their lives together, hoping that he will hear her and regain consciousness. "Billy, are you with me?" She has trouble speaking. Tears catch in her throat. "Billy, I'm with you—all the way!" A tear rolls down her cheek. It lands on Billy's forehead and rolls into his eye. The tear grows larger and Billy stares into it. It is filled with happy memories of days gone by. In his mind, Billy hears Strawberry singing the prettiest of songs.

Let me take you down, 'cause
I'm goin' to
Strawberry Fields
Nothing is real and nothing to
get hung about
Strawberry Fields forever.
Living is easy with eyes closed.
Misunderstanding all you see
It's getting hard to be someone
but it all works out
It doesn't matter much to me.

Let me take you down, 'cause I'm
goin' to
Strawberry Fields
Nothing is real and nothing to get
hung about
Strawberry Fields forever.

No one I think is in my tree
I mean it must be high or low
That is, you know you can't tune
in but it's all right
That is I think it's not too bad

Let me take you down, 'cause I'm
goin' to
Strawberry Fields

Nothing is real and nothing to
    get hung about
Strawberry Fields forever

Always know, sometimes think it's
    me
But you know I know and it's a
    dream
I think I know of thee, ah yes,
    but it's all wrong
That is I think I disagree.

Let me take you down, 'cause I'm
    goin' to
Strawberry Fields
Nothing is real and nothing to
    get hung about
Strawberry Fields forever.

Billy lies on a bed of the softest down; Strawberry's hair is flowing down over his face. "Billy,
what's the softest thing you've ever touched?"

He pulls her close to him. "You are," he whispers
in her ear. He places his fingertips on her ears,
then lets them slide slowly down her neck.

Suddenly another voice penetrates the haze.
"Baby, you touch me and I'll touch you!"

Billy feels nails digging into his back, as well as
teeth biting at his ears.

It must be Lucy.

He turns.

No, it's Strawberry. Then why is she acting like
Lucy? "Let me make you want me," she says as
she tears at his shirt. This can't be Strawberry! He
blinks and his sweet, soft Strawberry is gently
stroking his brow. "Billy, I'll be yours forever."

There is a voice behind him. There are two Strawberries, and one acts just like Lucy. Strawberry/Lucy pulls at him. "No, he's mine!"

Good Strawberry and evil Strawberry push and tear at him. Then they begin to beat each other. He falls to the ground, afraid to look up—afraid to see who has him.

Then he feels the soft kisses of Strawberry on his lips. Her soft hair gently brushes against his face.

Billy reaches up to kiss her lips once again. He opens his eyes. He really is kissing Strawberry. It's not a dream. She is his dream come true! He grabs her and gratefully pulls her to him.

At the far end of the van, Mark, Dave and Bob flirt once again with the computerettes. They desperately need an answer. "Where are the last two instruments?" they ask over and over again.

Bob tickles Martha; Mark fondles Irma's nuts and bolts; Dave whispers sweet nothings to Barbra. The only thing the videoscreen reveals is Billy lying in Strawberry's arms.

The computerettes hiss meanly at the screen. The hiss grows louder—louder—louder.

Mark is frantic. "They're jealous of Strawberry!"

The boys work harder and harder to convince the computerettes there is no need for anger.

Dave pleads with Barbra. "Pay no attention to Billy. He doesn't realize how sensuous a computer can be!"

"What can she give him?" snarls Barbra. "I can rub your back, cook your dinner and figure out your taxes all at the same time!"

Mark pleads: "It's true, Irma! I'm crazy about you!"

But the computerettes grow more and more red-faced. There will be no more help from them. They've had it with these heartless Heartlanders, none of whom really wants a computerette bride, no matter how hard they pretend.

Mark polishes Irma's wire hair. "Now, isn't this better than your waiting on Mr. Mustard?"

"It is."

Bob rubs Martha's neck. "I've never known such happiness before!" he says sweetly.

She beeps contentedly. "You don't really mean that," she teases.

Dave reads Barbra a story as she lies back with her bulbs out and her feet up. "Once upon a time, in the deep, dark, cold forest, there was this . . ." With Barbra's bulbs out, he tries to turn the knobs on the videoscreen.

Barbra suddenly snaps, "You're full of it, buster! You're always trying to get me where I live. But you're not getting me anymore!"

Martha begins to beat Bob on the chest. "You lied to me! You never did want that home in the country!"

Irma starts beating up on Mark. "How could you take advantage of me, you transistor-breaker?"

The computerettes stand tall and erect.

Barbra raps for attention. "Irma, Martha, we are no longer an asset to our profession. We have shamed ourselves by helping these cutie cads."

The computerettes grow rigidly tense. They seem to be holding their breath. Suddenly, flashes of light come from their bulb eyes; smoke seeps from their speaker mouths; their bodies start to shake violently.

The boys run for cover.

The computerettes self-destruct in a blaze of

fiery circuits, squeaks and squeals. They lie shattered all over the van.

There is a long, stunned pause.

The boys are panic-stricken. What are they going to do? Smoke is everywhere. Everyone is overcome with fits of coughing.

Billy opens the cupboard hoping to find something—anything that will cut the smoke. Nothing. He looks under the sink. Lo and behold! It's Sgt. Pepper's bass drum!

Billy holds it victoriously over his head. Everyone jumps up and down for joy.

Now they are missing only *one* instrument. If only they could find it, Heartland would be safe once again.

They look at the broken computerettes on the floor. Will they ever find the last instrument? And what if they don't? They stare at the broken computerettes and feel as if their own hearts had been broken.

ELEVEN

In B.D.'s inner office, B.D., Lucy and Dougie pace back and forth, preoccupied with their own thoughts.

Dougie bumps into B.D.

B.D. gives him a dirty look. He growls, "This idea of yours had better work. I've had to cancel a month's worth of concerts. That's a six-million-dollar gross down the drain! *You'll* be down the drain if your idea doesn't work."

B.D. continues pacing back and forth.

"Trust me, B.D.," replies Dougie. "I have as much to lose as you do. That's why it'll work!"

Lucy shrieks, "You two think you're the only ones who have anything to lose! I'm in this for money, not love! And I'm not seeing a cent!"

The Diamonds dash in from the outer waiting room. "They're here!" they shriek. "They're here!"

B.D. gathers his wits. "Calm down!" he coaxes. "Just calm down!"

Billy, Mark, Dave, Bob and Strawberry walk disheartedly into the room.

Dougie and B.D. greet them with a round of hugs and kisses.

"We know how you are suffering," Dougie tells Billy. "We are, too. Who would have believed that anyone would want to hurt Heartland?"

In Dougie's heart, it could not have happened soon enough.

Strawberry stares at the posters on the walls of B.D.'s office. Each poster announces a Lonely Hearts Club Band concert in a major city. Each has the word CANCELLED stenciled over it.

"But we have a surprise for you—something that will surely make you feel better." Dougie grins. He unfurls a new poster across B.D.'s desk. It shows a weeping Mr. Kite standing in front of a Mustardized Heartland. The poster reads:

THE BENEFIT FOR MR. KITE
FEATURING SGT. PEPPER'S
LONELY HEARTS CLUB BAND

The words SOLD OUT are stenciled across this one in big, bright, bold letters.

"It may not save Heartland," explains Dougie, "but it will raise money for a national search for the last instrument. We'll also release an album. All that money will be poured into the search also. You will also cheer up Heartland—and Heartland needs cheering up badly. It's something we've all got to do!"

"It's a wonderful idea!" gasps Billy. "We should have thought of it sooner!"

The boys pat Dougie on the back.

Strawberry throws her arms around Dougie. "Dougie, thank you! You do have a good heart, after all!" Dougie holds her tightly.

Dougie shows them a flock of leaflets. They read:

LET'S MAKE MR. KITE SMILE AGAIN

and:

HELP US CHEER UP HEARTLAND

B.D. puts a fatherly arm around Billy. "We're going to cheer up Heartland. It's the most important thing we can hope to do!"

"Now, go rehearse," says Dougie. "You haven't played in a long time. Get set to put on your best show." More hugs. Then the group dashes eagerly from the room.

Lucy triumphantly stretches out on the couch. "What suckers they are!" She laughs. "Boy, is goodness dumb!"

B.D. pours three glasses of champagne and B.D., Lucy and Dougie merrily clink their glasses together. "I love a benefit," toasts B.D., "especially when the benefit is for us!"

Even at its worst, the anticipation of the return of Sgt. Pepper's Lonely Hearts Club Band brings back a spark of life to the dying town of Heartland.

Baker George cleans the soot from his bakery windows. The brashy boys do their best to clear the streets of garbage. Teacher Ellen and her students plant flowers in the neglected flowerbeds. Each day the anticipation grows.

And a few days later, the world's most famous rock group does arrive. *THE LONELY HEARTS CLUB BAND IS BACK!!*

The band eagerly sings a number it has written just for this occasion:

For the benefit of Mr. Kite
There will be a show tonight on
    trampoline
The Hendersons will all be there
Late of Pablo Fanques Fair,
    what a scene!
Over men and horses, hoops and
    garters
Lastly through a hogshead of
    real fire!
In this way, Mr. K. will
    challenge the world!
The celebrated Mr. K.
Performs his feat on Saturday
    at Bishopgate
The Hendersons will dance and sing
As Mr. Kite flies through the ring
    ... don't be late.

Messrs. K. and H. assure the
    public
Their production will be second to
    none
And of course, Henry the Horse
    dances the waltz!
The band begins at ten to six
When Mr. K. performs his tricks
    without a sound. ...

And Mr. H. will demonstrate
Ten somersets he'll undertake
    on solid ground. ...

Having been some days in
preparation
A splendid time is guarant.ed
for all.
And tonight Mr. Kite is topping
the bill.

Mr. Mustard's van is driven by Strawberry into
Heartland's town square as the boys perform on
top of it. They are majestically dressed in white
marching band costumes, and they play with all
the power and magic they possess. Suddenly
Heartland's heart beats once again.

The silly girls boogie with the brashy boys; Old
Lady Pearl merrily wheels herself after the band;
the children chase each other around the huge
Greasy Mustard Burger. Everyone feels happy
once again.

Horses waltz down the street; cows dance in
time to the music; dogs and cats strut to the beat.

The Sgt. Pepper weathervane unbends itself
and smiles down at the town it loves. These people are good, it thinks, and their goodness must be
preserved!

The silly girls and brashy boys dance toward
Heartland City Hall. Mr. Kite stands on the steps
of the Museum. Even though he is eighty-two, and
it's not yet sunset, his favorite time of day, he
performs a dozen perfect somersaults!

Billy searches the crowd for his parents. So do
Strawberry and Mark, Dave and Bob. They all
spot them at the same time.

There are hugs and tears and kisses. Ernest and
Saralinda embrace their son. Ernest is proud.
"Billy's come to bring happiness back to Heart-
land!"

Linda and Stuart Fields kiss Strawberry. Linda weeps. "We forgive you for leaving home."

Zena and Bill hold their sons close to them. Zena feels faint. "I'm glad you're all back! This is where you belong!"

Everyone will sleep easier this night. After all, Heartland's favorite children have come home.

That night Billy and Strawberry sit under the giant Greasy Mustard Burger searching the heavens for stars.

"It's good to be home," says Billy. "It's good to be home with you."

They hold hands and walk toward the Shears' barn. Once again, Strawberry falls asleep in Billy's arms there. But this time she knows she is not being watched. And so she sleeps peacefully, with a smile of love and contentment on her face.

The following evening, Heartland's town square is crowded with people. Not since Woodstock have so many stars been gathered for one occasion.

Fans are everywhere. They sit on rooftops and poke their heads out of windows to search for comfortable spots for viewing.

Strawberry stands on the porch of the Home for Our Beloved Aged. She smiles proudly. This is Heartland—the way it should be.

Huge klieg lights scan the town. They play off the shiny surface of the Heartland Hot-Air Balloon, put on display for this very special occasion.

Billy, Mark, Dave, Bob and Mr. Kite sit onstage in a special box of honor. Mr. Kite is the emcee. "And now, it is my pleasure to present Earth, Wind and Fire!"

The crowd cheers as Mr. Kite shakes the hands of this brilliant group. Then Earth, Wind and Fire begins to wow the crowd.

Earth, Wind and Fire decides to honor the Lonely Hearts Club Band by playing one of that band's biggest hits.

I was alone, I took a ride
I didn't know what I would find there
Another road, where maybe I
  could see another kind of life there
Ooh, then I suddenly see you.
Ooh, did I tell you I need you
Every single day of my life?

Got to get you in to my life!
Got to get you in to my life!

You didn't run, you didn't lie
You knew I wanted just to hold you
And had you gone, you knew in time
  we'd meet again for I'd have told you
Ooh, you were meant to be near me
Ooh, and I want you to hear me
Say we'll be together every day

Got to get you in to my life!
Got to get you in to my life!

What can I do, what can I be
When I'm with you, I want to stay there
If I'm true, I'll never leave
  and if I do I know the way there
Ooh, then I suddenly see you
Ooh, did I tell you I need you
Every single day of my life?

Got to get you in to my life!
Got to get you in to my life!

Mr. Mustard and Brute sit in the back seat of the cab as it races toward Heartland.

Mustard leans forward, pumping his body back and forth as if he were a rudder that could increase the speed of the car. "Faster! Take short-cuts! Faster!" he screams at the driver.

The driver is an aging Hollywood extra who once doubled for Percy Kilbride in *Ma and Pa Kettle Go to Waikiki*. He's not taking any guff. "Cool it. I once was in the movies, you know," he says to Mustard. "And you look like a loser to me!"

B.D. sits in the Heartland Hardware Store, which has been converted into a makeshift recording studio. The tapes are running, recording the entire Benefit for Mr. Kite for the benefit of B.D. Brockhurst. With him is the pasty-faced, heavily Braggi-ed Evil Gladiola.

"First there's the money from the tickets for the concert. Then I'll make a million—no, *millions*—from this album. Damn—I should have hired a camera crew and made a documentary!" B.D. pulls at his hair. "Damn! Damn!"

"Don't worry," soothingly replies the Evil Gladiola. "I've stolen everybody's royalties today. They're in an unnumbered Swiss bank account. Meanwhile we can always fire a few secretaries for using too many paper clips. You know how fastidious and cheap I am with the little people. I make them suffer just for you. I'll torture anybody to look good in your eyes!"

"I have to go to the bathroom," says B.D.

His limousine pulls up. B.D. never goes to the

bathroom without taking his limousine. He usually keeps one car and driver in every room of every house or hardware store he is in.

The cab roars down the highway.

Mr. Mustard's nostrils flare; his eyes bulge. "I'll get my revenge, and I'll get Strawberry too!" he declares.

He can see it now: Strawberry and he happily sharing a hot dog bathed in mustard—Strawberry at one end, he at the other, both anxiously chewing toward the middle. . . .

The cab leaps up into the air. Mustard bumps his head on the roof. He punches Brute in the face. "You dummy!"

Brute looks hurt. "Gee, boss, I'm not even driving! Do you want me to drive? Is that it? Huh . . . huh?"

Mustard punches him again. "Shut up!"

Dougie and Lucy stealthily sneak into the Heartland Museum. Their eyes dart expectantly around the room. There in the corner are huge sacks of money, the proceeds from the Benefit for Mr. Kite. Lucy bends down and holds one of the sacks to her breasts. She moans with ecstasy. "Who needs B.D.," she laughs, "when I've got you!"

Dougie laughs wildly. They fall into each other's arms.

Dougie opens a sack and dumps the bills over Lucy. She rolls around in money, stuffing the bills into her clothes, rubbing them over her body, groaning with delight.

She grabs Dougie and stuffs the bills into his clothes, all the while laughing wildly.

Dougie joins in the mad laughter. For the first

time in his life, a woman is crazy for him, and she's terrific! "You're right—who needs B.D.?"

She whispers loudly in his ear, "With all this cash, we could go away. You and I could leave B.D. and never look back!"

Dougie grabs her excitedly. "Yes! Oh, yes!"

"Steal the money for me!" she growls.

"Yes, yes!" Dougie replies again, kissing her all over.

"Now!" she demands.

He'll do it and then he'll have his woman—a spectacular one! A woman who once loved Billy Shears! He begins to tie the sacks of money together.

A song rolls around in Lucy's mind:

> You never give me your money
> You only give me your funny paper
> And in the middle of negotiations
>   you break down.
>
> I never give you my number
> I only give you my situation
> And in the middle of investigation
>   I break down
>
> Out of college, money spent
> See no future, pay no rent
> All the money's gone, nowhere
>   to go
> Any jobber got the sack
> Monday morning, turning back
> Yellow lorry slow, nowhere to go
>
> But, oh, that magic feeling,
>   nowhere to go

Oh, that magic feeling, nowhere
   to go
Nowhere to go.

One sweet dream
Pick up the bags and get in the
   limousine
Soon, we'll be away from here
Step on the gas and wipe that
   tear away
One sweet dream came true today
Came true today.

One, two, three, four, five, six,
   seven
All good children go to heaven
One, two, three, four, five, six,
   seven
All good children go to heaven
One, two, three, four, five, six,
   seven
All good children go to heaven. ....

The cab pulls up to Heartland town square.
Mustard and Brute jump out. The fare is one
thousand five hundred sixty-three dollars and thirty
cents. Mustard pays it. He gives the driver a
nickel tip.

Stealthily, Mustard and Brute sneak into town.
Mustard gloats to himself. "I'm back, Heartland—
and this time it's to stay! Mustardville will be
mine—and so will Strawberry!"

He watches the people crowded around the
town square cheering the entertainers. Soon he
will be Mayor of their fair town and they will
cheer him. "Long live Mustard! Long live Mustard!"

They prowl quietly behind the Heartland Home for Our Beloved Aged. Mustard suddenly spots Strawberry alone on the porch. Brute and he casually stroll over. Then Brute grabs her. He clamps his hand over her mouth and carries her into the shadows.

In Mustard's van, Brute ties Strawberry to a dollar-sign pole, the only thing he can find in the van. The pole had been a Christmas present from "FVB."

The computerettes, bruised and bandaged, but repaired and in working order, cheer her capture.

Suddenly Mr. Mustard discovers the cornet and the saxophone. He now has three of Pepper's instruments. He prances around the van with a demented grin on his face.

Suddenly Dougie throws open the van door, and Lucy and he begin dumping sacks of money into the van.

Brute reaches out. With one arm he grabs Lucy, with the other, Dougie.

Mustard scoops up the sacks. He rips one open and tosses the bills into the air. "I love it! The touch! The smell! It's so wonderful!" he trills.

A message appears on the videoscreen. Mustard, Brute, Dougie, Lucy, Irma, Barbra, Martha and a bound and gagged Strawberry study the screen.

BRING ALL INSTRUMENTS TO "FVB" IMMEDIATELY!

OUR ARMY IS ABOUT TO BE UNLEASHED!

THE WORLD WILL BE OURS!

REMEMBER, LOSERS CAN BE WINNERS!

Strawberry's eyes dash fearfully back and forth as she watches the others puff out their chests and slap each other on the back.

There is a religious expression on Mustard's face. "Step on the gas!" he bellows. "Soon the world will be ours!"

Earth, Wind and Fire finishes its last number as a panic-stricken Mrs. Fields climbs onto the stage. She dashes to Billy. "Strawberry's missing!" she exclaims. "I can't find her anywhere!"

Billy gets up and searches the crowd. Suddenly he sees the van pull away. He knows instantly: Mustard is back—and he's got Strawberry!

Mark, Dave, Bob and he dash from the edge of the stage. They must come to the rescue, and they must do it now.

They run across the field to the Heartland Hot-Air Balloon. They jump into it and the balloon takes off.

Beneath them the van barrels down the highway. On its roof Mustard looks at them through a spyglass as he curses them and shakes his fist.

He is the villain of villains, the boys think. They have no idea what's in store for them when they get to the lair of "FVB."

Mustard sits on the roof of his van at his breakfast table. A bound and gagged Strawberry faces him. At the table also are a bound and gagged Dougie and a bound and gagged Lucy.

The computerettes serve a lavish breakfast: freshly squeezed orange juice, curried eggs and bacon with a variety of hot rolls and jams, strawberries with fresh cream, and coffee.

Mustard spots that wretched balloon tailing

them in the sky, but what does it matter? Soon he will meet "FVB," and "FVB" will take care of him, as well as those dumb-dumbs in the balloon.

Mustard has never been in a happier mood. He decides to entertain his guests with one of his favorite numbers—a number that never earned him much applause.

When I get older losing my hair
Many years from now
Will you still be sending me a
    valentine
Birthday greeting, bottle of wine
If I'd been out till quarter to
    three
Would you lock the door?
Will you still need me, will you
    still feed me
When I'm sixty-four?
You'll be older too,
And if you say the word,
I could stay with you.

I could be handy, mending a fuse
When your lights have gone
You can knit a sweater by the
    fireside
Sunday morning go for a ride.
Doing the garden, digging the
    weeds
Who could ask for more?

Will you still need me?
Will you still feed me?
When I'm sixty-four!

Every summer we can rent a
     cottage in the Isle of Wight,
     if it's not too dear.
We shall scrimp and save
Grandchildren on your knee
Vera, Chuck, and Dave.

Send me a postcard, drop me
     a line
Stating point of view
Indicate precisely what you mean
     to say
Yours sincerely wasting away.

Give me your answer, fill in a
     form
Mine forever more
Will you still need me, will you
     still feed me
When I'm sixty-four.

A contented Mustard leans back to soak up the
sun. "The Story of the Marriage of Mr. Mustard
to Miss Strawberry Fields," he says out loud. And
then he spiels a tale of domestic bliss.

"Once upon a time, the sweet and lovely
Miss . . ."

Strawberry is strapped to an operating table in
Mustardstein's Castle. Then Dr. Mustardstein pulls
a switch. A million jolts of electricity go through
Strawberry. She sits up. The Bride of Mustardstein—ready to wreak havoc upon the world.

The image makes Mustard giggle.

Now she's Joan of Arc, and he is the execu-
tioner. Mustard drops the match. Smoke billows
up around his perspiring bride, tied to a stake.

"I can see the beautiful children we could have—you and I," he says adoringly. Three ugly little Mustard look-alikes ring the stake.

And then he envisions Strawberry starring in an old two-reeler. She is tied to railroad tracks. A train bears down on her. Mustard is so in love! He kneels before her, arms outstretched. "Tell me you need me," he begs, "or I'll let you die!"

What a peculiar kind of love!

High in the sky, Billy, Mark, Dave and Bob watch Mustard through binoculars.

"That fiend!" Billy gasps. "He's stuffing his face with strawberries!"

"And he's got Strawberry!" says Mark.

"I'll get him!" says Billy.

Suddenly the van swerves to the left and drives into a cave.

"That must be the lair!" says Billy.

"Soon we will know who is behind all this."

"I'm scared!" says Dave.

"I'm frightened!" says Mark.

"I'm nervous!" says Bob.

"So am I!" Billy says quietly. "So am I!"

TWELVE

Deep in the cave is an arena, exactly the same size and shape as Madison Square Garden. Its stands are filled with silent, mesmerized, brain-washed youths dressed in brown shorts and brown shirts. They sit silently under huge dollar-bill pennants. Their glazed, vacant eyes stare down at the center of the arena. In its center is a giant pyramid of money. Hundreds of youths wheel in barrel after barrel of money and paste the money onto the pyramid much the way wallpaper is attached to walls.

On top of the pyramid is Sgt. Pepper's tuba. Above it a sign flashes nonstop. It reads:

WE HATE LOVE.

WE HATE JOY.

WE LOVE MONEY.

REMEMBER, LOSERS CAN BE WINNERS!

The audience slowly shakes its head in agreement. Finally the lights in the arena dim. Then a band takes to the stage. It is "FVB."

There's been AWB, the Average White Band; ELO, the Electric Light Orchestra; CSN, Crosby, Stills, and Nash; BST, Blood, Sweat, and Tears; but there had never been anything like FVB, the Future Villain Band, starring Sal Futurevillain.

This band is the most unknown band in the entire history of the world—and the most disliked. They are meaner, more tuneless and more arrogant than any other band has ever been.

Year after year, this band played gig after gig in small clubs and everyone always booed and hated them!

Do you know what ten years of failure in rock 'n' roll can do to you? Ten years of small clubs and no pay and being told you're a loser by promoters and audiences alike? Ten years of record company presidents telling you that you are lousy, your music sucks and you should pack it up and go home? Something in your head snaps.

FVB and its lead singer, Sal Futurevillain, continue to play wildly on top of the pyramid. Sal may be smelly and filthy and have pins in his nose and a loose screw in his head, but he is smart— very smart! He was a major in psychology and computer technology and had graduated with honors—a brilliant boy! But all he wanted was rock 'n' roll. And that was the one thing he couldn't have. It had made him crazy!

He also had rich parents—parents who gave him anything so long as he didn't play that rotten music at home.

Sal Futurevillain decided to use his superior academic skills and his parents' wealth to brainwash himself the largest audience ever in the history of rock.

Computer readouts showed him that the easiest targets for this brainwashing were "losers," those who were unloved and had failed in their careers. Sal had set out to find the most unloved failures in the country.

He was succeeding mightily. Then one day an old history book told him about the magic of Sgt. Pepper's musical instruments.

He had sent that idiot Mustard—a super-loser if ever there was one—after them. Surprise of surprises, Mustard had indeed stolen them. And the biggest surprise of all? The instruments did have magical powers! With them, he could brainwash millions!

Now Sal Futurevillain had an army. He was also reaping tons of money and his audience was growing by leaps and bounds. Soon he would unleash this army on the world; they would wreak havoc and he would punish everyone for denying him the pleasures of superstardom. That will teach 'em, he thought, for not recognizing that ugly is as good as beautiful, mediocrity is as commendable as talent, and that losers can be winners too!

Bathed in a harsh, cold spotlight, Sal is an extremely tall, pathetically thin, extremely unattractive creature as he barbarically dances on top of the pyramid.

"A-one, a-two, a-one-two-three!" he screams. The Future Villain Band begins to play! Never has a more horrible sound been made by any group in rock 'n' roll.

Sal begins to scream a number that he is sure will become a hit if the world only knew bad from good.

Here come old flat top
He come grooving up slowly
He got Joo Joo eyeball
He one holyroller
He got hair down to his knee
Got to be a joker, he just
   do what he please
He wear no shoeshine
He got toe jam football
He got monkey finger
He shoot Coca-Cola
He say I know you, you know me
One thing I can tell you is you
   got to be free
Come together, right now, over me.

He bag productions
He got walrus gumboot
He got-o-no sideboard
He one spinal cracker
He got feet down below his knee ...
Hold in his armchair you can
   feel his disease
Come together, right now, over me.

RIGHT ...
He got roller coaster
He got early warning
He got muddy water
He one mojo filter
He say one and one and one is
   three
Got to be good-looking 'cause
   he so hard to see
Come together, right now, over me.

During a musical break, Sal screams out over the racket to the glazed crowd. "I was once a loser! I used the most advanced technology to determine who the other losers were! I joined these losers together to prove that losers can be winners! And winners we will be today when all these losers join together with me!"

Mustard and Brute and Dougie and Lucy scurry down the aisles of the arena. They carry Sgt. Pepper's bass drum, cornet and saxophone. They also carry Strawberry, who is still tied to the dollar sign. They scale the money pyramid until they reach the top.

Mustard offers the instruments to Sal Futurevillain while Brute plants the dollar stake bearing Strawberry into the huge mound of money. She is about to be offered up to a fate worse than death! She will be Sal Futurevillain's groupie!

Sal glares at Mustard. The trembling Mustard looks up at him, then begins to kiss the hem of his tattered denim jeans. A spotlight scans the full set of Sgt. Pepper's instruments. Sal turns up the volume; he screeches a tune of triumph. He has won!

The glazed audience comes alive with excitement; they frantically sing and dance in the stands. Then they joyfully hit each other over the head and punch each other in the jaw. The instruments make Sal's dream come true. These brainwashed zombies are convinced that FVB is the best rock band ever! FVB makes them feel good, and when they feel good they become mean!

Billy, Mark, Dave and Bob have no trouble getting into the arena. All the guards are busy boogying to the music made by FVB.

Billy gulps. There's Strawberry looking like Jane tied to a stake in a Tarzan movie.

Billy spots Sgt. Pepper's instruments on top of the pyramid. He is amazed that the audience loves this vile, vile band!

Billy, Mark, Dave and Bob run down the aisle. They push the screaming fans aside and scale the pyramid.

Billy heads for Strawberry, but Mustard blocks his way. Billy flattens him out with one blow.

Sal Futurevillain glares at the intruders. "Get outta here! This is my gig!" He scowls. "Would you climb onstage for The Stones, The Who or Led Zeppelin?"

Billy replies, "You've devastated my homeland, Heartland!"

"A minor crime in order to achieve major superstardom!" Sal glares at Billy. "Kill him!" he orders. "Kill him because he's nice!"

Billy hurls himself on the lead singer and begins to throttle him. This is indeed a fight to the death. Billy falls on his back. Sal grabs Billy's throat and strangles him mercilessly. Billy hangs over the pyramid, gasping for breath. Then he rears up and Futurevillain lands on his back!

The maddened musicians get up and begin to swing wildly. Billy heads for Sal, and Sal knows Billy can take him. Will he be a god no longer? He will punish Billy for intruding. Sal picks up the dollar-sign stake bearing Strawberry, waves it around his head, and then hurls it from the pyramid. Down and down it goes until it lands at the base of the pyramid. Strawberry lies battered and dead!

"No!" Billy screams. "No!"

Sal then grabs Billy by the throat. Suddenly,

Billy has the strength of one hundred men. He lifts Sal Futurevillain over his head and hurls him from the pyramid. Sal lands directly on the stake, his face a mere inch from Strawberry's.

Billy lets out a bloodcurdling scream! Who knew it would ever come to this?

THIRTEEN

In Heartland, Strawberry's glass coffin is laid out on the Heartland bandstand. The entire coffin is covered with flowers. Sgt. Pepper's instruments rest at the side of the stage.

Dressed in black, Billy kneels at the coffin. He whispers to his dead love, "If I had never told you I loved you, I love you more today than I ever did." A single tear rolls down his face.

In his mind, Billy sings a farewell to Strawberry:

> Once there was a way to get back homeward
> Once there was a way to get back home
> Sleep pretty darling, do not cry
> And I will sing a lullaby
> Golden slumbers fill your eyes
> Smiles awake you when you rise.

176

> Sleep pretty darling do not cry
> And I will sing a lullaby
> Once there was a way to get back
>   homeward
> Once there was a way to get back
>   home
> Sleeep pretty darling, do not cry
> And I will sing a lullaby.

All of Heartland is dressed in black. The towns-folk ring the town square. Their heads are all bowed, as is the head of the Sgt. Pepper weather-vane.

The coffin is laid in a hearse, and as the church bell tolls, the hearse heads up the hill toward Heartland Cemetery. A weeping Billy walks behind the coffin. The entire town follows behind him.

They sing as they prepare to bury Strawberry:

> Boy, you're gonna carry that weight
> Carry that weight a long time
> Boy, you're gonna carry that weight
> Carry that weight a long time
>
> I never give you my pillow
> I only send you my invitations
> And in the middle of the celebrations
> I break down.

At the gravesite Strawberry is lowered into the ground.

The Heartlanders weep and moan. This is the worst day of their lives. They wonder how they will ever recover.

"I'll never have a happy story to tell again," Mr. Kite mutters. "Happiness is gone forever!"

Billy covers his face with his hands. Trembling, he gets up and walks away from the grave.

Mark puts his arm around Billy's shoulders, but Billy turns away. He begins to run. He must be alone with his grief. He runs and runs until he can run no longer. He sinks to his knees and bursts into a series of convulsive sobs.

Finally, he is able to get up again. Slowly, he heads toward Heartland's town square.

The love theme he had once composed for Strawberry plays frantically in his mind:

> The long and winding road that
>   leads to your door
> Will never disappear, I've seen
>   that road before
> It always leads me here
> Leads me to your door
>
> The wild and windy night that
>   the rain has washed away
> Has left a pool of tears crying
>   for the day
> Why leave me standing here
> Let me know the way.
>
> Many times I've been alone, and
>   many times I've cried
> Anyway you'll never know the many
>   ways I've tried
> But still they lead me back to the
>   long, winding road
> You left me standing here, a long,
>   long time ago

Don't leave me waiting here
Lead me to your door

But still they lead me back to the
long, winding road
You left me standing here, a long,
long time ago
Don't leave me waiting here
Lead me to your door

He crosses the town square and comes to the Heartland Home for Our Beloved Aged. He opens the door and steps into the building. He heads for Strawberry's bedroom.

"So many times I have walked up to your door to surprise you and kiss you and I never thought that one day you might not be here," he says out loud.

He enters the room. He looks at the photographs that decorate the room. There he is, his arm around Strawberry as they walk in the fields. His body shakes as he falls onto her bed. He holds her pillow to his chest and weeps like a little boy. He cannot live without Strawberry.

There is a look of steely determination on his face. "I am with you now—all the way!"

Mark Henderson quietly composes a song that sums up his feelings about how rotten the world is when someone as beautiful as Strawberry dies:

I read the news today, oh boy
About a lucky man who made the grade
And though the news was rather sad
Well, I just had to laugh
I saw the photograph
He blew his mind out in a car

He didn't notice that the lights
    had changed
A crowd of people stood and stared
They've seen his face before
Nobody was really sure
If he was from the House of Lords
I saw a film today, oh boy
The English Army had just won the war
A crowd of people turned away
But I just had to look
Having read the book
I'd love to turn you on.
Woke up, fell out of bed
Dragged a comb across my head
Found my way downstairs and drank
    a cup
And looking up I noticed I was
    late
Found my coat and grabbed my hat
Made the bus in seconds flat
Found my way upstairs and had
    a smoke
Somebody spoke and I went into
    a dream
I read the news today, oh boy
Four thousand holes in Blackburn,
    Lancashire
And though the holes were rather
    small
They had to count them all
Now they know how many holes it
    takes to fill the Albert Hall.

Billy walks to Strawberry's window and throws it open. He stands on the ledge, staring down at the ground. Then he jumps.

The Sgt. Pepper weathervane gasps as Billy takes the plunge.

A violent wind comes up. The Sgt. Pepper weathervane spins faster and faster. Suddenly, it isn't a weathervane at all. *Sgt. Pepper has come to life!*

Sgt. Pepper points his finger at the Heartland Home for Our Beloved Aged, and begins to sing:

> . . .
> Get back, get back, get back to
>   where you once belonged.
> Get back, get back, get back to
>   where you once belonged.
>
> Get back Loretta
> Your mommy is waiting for you
> Wearing high heel shoes and
>   her low neck sweater
> Get back home, Loretta
> Get back, get back, get back to
>   where you once belonged.
> Get back.

Billy suddenly flies back in through the window. Astonished, he stares at his grandfather, who merrily waves back at his grandson.

"Happy endings, Billy! I'm a firm believer in happy endings!" proclaims the legendary Sergeant.

Pepper then dances down the front of the building and crosses the town square. With each step he takes, Heartland comes miraculously back to life! The air is once again clean and crisp; gone are the garbage and graffiti. The sound of children laughing is heard everywhere.

Sgt. Pepper stands on the Heartland bandstand.

He spots Mustard's van and points his finger at it. There is a clap of thunder. The van collapses to reveal Mustard, who has been converted into an altar boy.

Pepper spots Lucy and Dougie Shears. He points his finger again. Lucy is now a nun and Dougie is a priest.

"Do only good!" he orders the converted trio.

He points his finger at the Heartland Hardware Store. B.D. and the Evil Gladiola are busy making bootleg tapes. There is a crack of thunder. B.D. has been turned into a young, unemployed vacuum-cleaner salesman from Peoria, and the Evil Gladiola is now a cheaply made T-shirt that reads: STAMP OUT GREED!

Sgt. Pepper glares at B.D. "I'm giving you a chance to become a mogul once again," he tells him, "but this time, do it right!"

Sgt. Pepper points his finger once again. The newly dug ground at Heartland Cemetery rises, then miraculously begins to part. Strawberry's coffin flies open; Strawberry steps out—alive, beautiful and young once again.

Billy can't believe his eyes. He scoops her into his arms.

Sgt. Pepper hugs his grandson and soon-to-be granddaughter. He stands on the bandstand next to Billy, Mark, Dave and Bob. They all begin to play. The Heartlanders pour into the town square at the sound of the music. They are all dressed in black.

Sgt. Pepper smiles. There is a crash of thunder. "Be the stars of your dreams," says Sgt. Pepper. And suddenly they are! In their imaginations, they are all the stars who have made music great.

Stars like: Stevie Wonder, The Rolling Stones,

The Who, Led Zeppelin, Aretha Franklin, Elton
John, David Bowie, Diana Ross, Fleetwood
Mac, The Average White Band, Brook Benton,
The Bay City Rollers, The Beach Boys, Elvin
Bishop, Shirley Bassey, The Captain and Tennille,
Joan Baez, Natalie Cole, Burt Bacharach, The
Electric Light Orchestra, Frankie Avalon, Barry
Manilow, The Association, Olivia Newton-John,
Paul Anka, Patti Smith, The Animals, Bruce
Springsteen, Herb Alpert, Barry White, and The
Allman Brothers.

They are also: Chuck Berry, Judy Collins, Blood,
Sweat, and Tears, Joe Cocker, Booker T. and The
M.G.'s, The Coasters, Pat Boone, Petula Clark,
Bread, Chicago, James Brown, Cheech and Chong,
Buffalo Springfield, Chubby Checker, Eric Burdon,
Ray Charles, Jerry Butler, The Byrds, Chad and
Jeremy, Glenn Campbell, David Cassidy, and Vicki
Carr.

And Dolly Parton, Charlie Pride, Liza Minnelli,
Johnny Mathis, Dusty Springfield, Brenda Lee,
Tanya Tucker, Thelma Huston, Jimmy Rogers,
Eddie Arnold, Charlie Rich, Don Cherry, Buck
Owens, Lynn Anderson, Doug Kershaw, Jessi
Colter, Sonny James, Roy Clark, Hoyt Axton, Don-
na Fargo, Gene Autry, Crystal Gayle, Merle Hag-
gard, and Tennessee Ernie Ford.

And Sam Cooke, Flo and Eddie, Rita Coolidge,
Roberta Flack, Jim Croce, The Fifth Dimension,
Crosby, Stills, Nash, and Young, Jose Feliciano,
Bobby Darin, Fabian, Mac Davis, The Everly
Brothers, Sammy Davis, Jr., John Denver, Duane
Eddie, Jackie DeShannon, The Eagles, Neil Dia-
mond, Dion, The Doors, Fats Domino, Donovan,
Leo Sayer, Nancy Wilson, Frankie Valli, Dean
Martin, Dick Haymes, Eddie Kendricks, Alice

Faye, Eddie Fisher, Mario Lanza, Debbie Reynolds, Teresa Brewer, Helen O'Connell, Oscar Petersen, Fanny Brice, Grace Moore, Mel Torme, Morgana King, Maurice Chevalier, and Nat King Cole.

And The Four Seasons, Ramsey Lewis, The Four Tops, Kris Kristofferson, Connie Francis, Gladys Knight and The Pips, Art Garfunkel, Carole King, Marvin Gaye, B. B. King, Bobbie Gentry, Janis Joplin, Leslie Gore, Tom Jones, Al Green, Janis Ian, The Jackson Five, The Hollies, Isaac Hayes, Quincy Jones, Bill Haley, Jimi Hendrix, and Engelbert Humperdinck.

And Gordon Lightfoot, Laura Nyro, Little Richard, Nilsson, Loggins and Messina, Wayne Newton, Trini Lopez, Randy Newman, Al Martino, Rick Nelson, Dave Mason, Johnny Nash, Don McLean, Anne Murray, Melanie, The Moody Blues, Sergio Mendez, Joni Mitchell, Bette Midler, and Buddy Miles.

And Roy Orbison, The McGuire Sisters, James Darren, The Lennon Sisters, The Brothers Four, Andy Gibb, Frank Zappa, Tony Orlando, Bing Crosby, Shaun Cassidy, Larry Gatlin, The Dave Clark Five, Rosemary Clooney, Michael Murphy, Manfred Mann, Hank Williams, Vaughn Monroe, Sarah Vaughan, Frankie Laine, Bill Monroe, Mose Allison, and Paul Williams.

And Neil Sedaka, Peter and Gordon, Seals and Crofts, Pink Floyd, Tommy Sands, Gene Pitney, Leon Russell, The Platters, Linda Ronstadt, The Pointer Sisters, Kenny Rogers, Bobby Rydell, Lloyd Price, Smokey Robinson, Gary Puckett and The Union Gap, Johnny Rivers, Otis Redding, Helen Reddy, and The Righteous Brothers.

And Patti Page, Dorothy Collins, Dave Brubeck, The Modernaires, Martha and The Vandellas, Kate

Smith, The Four Freshmen, The Mills Brothers, The Hi Los, Van Morrison, June Carter, June Christy, Russ Columbo, The Big Bopper, Carmen Lombardo, and Chet Baker.

And Bobby Sherman, Conway Twitty, Paul Simon, Tina Turner, Carly Simon, Tiny Tim, Frank Sinatra, Three Dog Night, Sly and the Family Stone, The Temptations, O. C. Smith, The Supremes, Sonny and Cher, Barbra Streisand, The Spinners, Rod Stewart, Cat Stevens, and James Taylor.

And Procol Harum, The Drifters, Steely Dan, The Moonglows, Traffic, The Spaniels, Cream, The O'Jays, The Jazz Crusaders, Manhattan Transfer, Hot Chocolate, Credence Clearwater Revival, Freddie Hubbard, Boz Scaggs, Weather Report, Hall and Oates, Shakti, Tom Waits, Bobby Vee, Duke Ellington, The Ventures, Louie Prima and Keely Smith, Bobby Vinton, Perry Como, War, Louis Armstrong, Jack Jones, and Andy Williams.

And Abba, Elvis Costello, Crazy Horse, Dennis Roussos, The Amazing Rhythm Aces, Crack the Sky, Alec Costandinos, Bob James, Angel, England Dan & John Ford Coley, The Climax Blues Band, The Isley Brothers, Ashford and Simson, Al Dimeola, Chic Corea, Beverly Sills, Atlanta Rhythm Section, Walter Egan, Stanley Clarke, Vladimir Horowitz, Yvonne Elliman, Jimmy Buffett, Dan Hill, The Band, Foreigner, B. T. Express, Emmy Lou Harris, George Benson, Michael Franks, Peter Brown, Robert Gordon, Leif Garrett, Bootsy's River Band, Andrew Gold, Blondie, and Debby Boone.

And Karla Bonoff, The Jefferson Starship, Lou Reed, Lou Rawls, Merv Griffin, Garland Jeffreys, REO Speedwagon, The Ramones, The Tubes, Waylon Jennings, Renaissance, Queen, The Tramps,

Billy Joel, Rufus, Player, Tower of Power, Journey, The Salsoul Orchestra, Parliament, Sweet, Kansas, Santa Esmeralda, Robert Palmer, Donna Summer, Lonnie Liston-Smith, The Outlaws, Stargard, Nick Lowe, Odyssey, The Manhattans, Lynyrd Skynyrd, Ralph MacDonald, Meatloaf, Ted Nugent, Maria Muldaur, and Eddie Money.

And Van Halen, Jerry Vale, The Village People, Matt Monroe, Bob Welch, Edith Piaf, Foghat, Johnny Almond, Wings, Joni James, Grover Washington, Jr., Lainie Kazan, Judy Garland, Wha-Koo, Nico, Link Wray, Vic Damone, Jay & The Americans, Julius La Rosa, Don Ho, Melissa Manchester, Gil Scott Heron, Hamilton, Joe Frank & Reynolds, Lambert Hendrix & Ross, Jimmy Reed, Roger Miller, Mylon LeFevre, Dan Fogelberg, Lulu, Mike Douglas, The Rascals, Charles Aznavour, Roberta Sherwood, KC & The Sunshine Band, Jimmy Boyd, Donnie & Marie Osmond, Hank Snow, Lonnie Donnigan, and Ry Cooder.

And Jimmy Osmond, Julie London, Barbi Benton, Wet Willie, Sam the Sham, Lord Buckley, Yusef Lateef, Journey, Dino, Desi & Billy, Roberta Peters, Patience & Prudence, Yes, Spanky & Our Gang, Lotte Lenya, Vicki Sue Robinson, Johnny Guitar Watson, Doc Watson, The Four Lads, Poco, Long John Baldry, Commander Cody, Delaney & Bonnie, Iron Butterfly, and Ezio Pinza.

And Chad Mitchell, Vanilla Fudge, Phil Ochs, Tom Paxton, Louden Wainwright III, Eartha Kitt, Georgia Gibbs, Lord Sutch, Frankie Lymon, Anita Bryant, Freddy & The Dreamers, Peter Allen, Guy Mitchell, Kitty Kalen, Nelson Eddy & Jeanette McDonald, Pacific Gas & Electric, Ben Vereen, Sylvia Sims, Bachman-Turner Overdrive, Johnny

Otis, Sir Lord Baltimore, Ronnie Blakely, Herman's Hermits, Focus, Mitch Ryder & The Detroit Wheels, Devo, James Brown, Johnnie Ray, Dinah Washington, Cozy Cole, The Penguins, Paul Horn, Cannonball Adderly, Alvin & The Chipmunks, Sister Sourire, and The New York Dolls.

And Carmen McRae, Dionne Warwicke, Judy Garland, Mary Wells, Ella Fitzgerald, Dinah Washington, Robert Goulet, Al Wilson, Henry Mancini, Jackie Wilson, Tony Bennett, Bill Withers, Percy Faith, Jethro Tull, Phoebe Snow, Dan Hicks and The Hot Licks, and Little Feat.

And Jerry Reed, Peggy Lee, Ray Price, Count Basie, Johnny Cash, Andre Previn, Jeannie C. Riley, Peter Nero, Al Hirt, Tammy Wynette, Chet Atkins, Burl Ives, Kingston Trio, Billy Paul, Horace Heidt, Charlie Parker, Harry James, Fletcher Henderson, Sammy Kaye, Ma Rainey, Gene Krupa, Billie Holiday, Guy Lombardo, Carol Channing, Freddy Martin, and Pearl Bailey.

And Ozzie Nelson, Jo Stafford, Alvina Ray, Dinah Shore, Buddy Rich, The Andrews Sisters, Artie Shaw, Doris Day, Lawrence Welk, Bobbie Blue Bland, Loretta Lynn, Lionel Hampton, Willie Nelson, Benny Goodman, Harry Belafonte, Dizzy Gillespie, Muddy Waters, Billy Eckstine, Bill Evans, Eddie Duchin, Stan Getz, Tommy Dorsey, Stan Kenton, Jimmy Dorsey, Woody Herman, Xavier Cugat, and Miles Davis.

And Ethel Merman, Mary Martin, Les Brown, Gwen Verdon, Bert Parks, Spike Jones, Dr. John, Liberace, The Sex Pistols, Gotham, The Harlettes, John Lee Hooker, Tony Martin, Dennis Day, The Staple Singers, Thelonius Monk, Peter, Paul, and Mary, Buddy Holly, Gary Wright, John Mayall,

Etta James, Jimmy Cliff, Bob Marley, Minnie Pearl, Keith Jarrett, Chuck Mangione, Bryan Ferry, Ten Years After, Black Sabbath, The Kinks, Jackson Browne, Heart, Kiss, and Bob Seger.

And Peter Frampton.

And The Bee Gees.

And George Burns.

And Paul Nicholas.

And Aerosmith.

And Alice Cooper.

And Earth, Wind and Fire.

And Steve Martin.

And Billy Preston.

And Elvis.

And The Beatles.

And many, many more.

Sgt. Pepper raises his baton. He smiles at Sgt. Pepper's Lonely Hearts Club Band, the biggest, the most talented, the happiest, the most loving band you will ever see.

No music will ever be sweeter than the music this band will make today.

Everybody joyously begins to sing. "One-two, one-two-three!"

It was twenty years ago today that
Sgt. Pepper taught the band
   to play
They've been going in and out of
   style
But they're guaranteed to raise
   a smile
So may I introduce to you
The act you've known for all these
   years
Sgt. Pepper's Lonely Hearts Club Band!

We're Sgt. Pepper's Lonely Hearts
  Club Band
We hope you will enjoy the show
We're Sgt. Pepper's Lonely Hearts
  Club Band
Sit back and let the evening go
Sgt. Pepper's Lonely, Sgt. Pepper's
  Lonely, Sgt. Pepper's Lonely Hearts
  Club Band.

It's wonderful to be here
It's certainly a thrill
You're such a lovely audience
We'd like to take you home with us
We'd love to take you home

I don't really want to stop the show
But I thought you might like to know
That the singer is going to sing a
  song
And he wants you all to sing along
So may I introduce to you
The one and only *BILLY SHEARS*

And Sgt. Pepper's Lonely Hearts
  Club Band!!!

We're Sgt. Pepper's Lonely Hearts
  Club Band
We hope you will enjoy the show
We're Sgt. Pepper's Lonely Hearts
  Club Band
Sit back and let the evening go
Sgt. Pepper's Lonely, Sgt. Pepper's
  Lonely, Sgt. Pepper's Lonely Hearts
  Club Band.

It's wonderful to be here
It's certainly a thrill
You're such a lovely audience
We'd like to take you home with us
We'd love to take you home

We're Sgt. Pepper's Lonely Hearts
  Club Band
We hope you have enjoyed the show
We're Sgt. Pepper's Lonely Hearts
  Club Band
We're sorry but it's time to go
Sgt. Pepper's Lonely, Sgt. Pepper's Lonely,
Sgt. Pepper's Lonely Hearts Club Band

We'd like to thank you once again
Sgt. Pepper's one and only
Lonely Hearts Club Band
It's getting very near the end
Sgt. Pepper's Lonely Hearts Club
  Band